A Baby for Christmas

Also by Keira Andrews

Contemporary

The Spy and the Mobster's Son
Honeymoon for One
Beyond the Sea
Ends of the Earth
Arctic Fire

Holiday

A Baby for Christmas
The Christmas Deal
The Christmas Leap
The Christmas Veto
Only One Bed
Merry Cherry Christmas
Santa Daddy
In Case of Emergency
Eight Nights in December
If Only in My Dreams
Where the Lovelight Gleams
Gay Romance Holiday Collection

Sports

Kiss and Cry
Reading the Signs
Cold War
The Next Competitor
Love Match
Synchronicity (free read!)

Gay Amish Romance Series

A Forbidden Rumspringa
A Clean Break

A Baby for

Christmas

BY KEIRA ANDREWS

A Baby for Christmas
Written and published by Keira Andrews
Cover by Dar Albert
Formatting by BB eBooks
Editing by Cecily Green

Acknowledgments

Many thanks to B and H for sharing their experiences with preemie infants. Thank you also to Cecily, Leslie, Lori, Mary, Rachel, and Rai for your help in bringing Cam and Jake's story to life!

Chapter One

CAM

THREE DAYS BEFORE another lonely Christmas, I discovered a baby's cry was unmistakable.

Carried on the bitter wind, the faint squall jolted me out of a daydream. Bonnie snorted and side-stepped, and I rubbed her chestnut mane as I leaned forward in the saddle.

What the holy hell?

I strained to listen, squinting beyond my herd of shaggy-haired yaks, who briefly lifted their wide heads at the sound before returning to business as usual. They chewed the long, yellowed grass poking up out of the thin layer of snow, their stony expressions and curved horns making them look a damn sight fiercer than they were.

Had the cry come from over toward the mountains? Noises loved to play tricks near the Rockies. I peered into the distance. Across the rolling, snow-dusted fields, beyond dense pine trees peppering the foothills, the white-capped peaks were hidden behind ominous gray clouds. More snow was coming.

A *lot* more.

I could taste the moisture in the air. Smell it. Feel it in my bones like truth, as dramatic as that sounded. But I *knew.* Though still below freezing, I'd been able to leave my woolen toque at home and wear my favorite black Stetson. The temperature had risen enough that instead of crystallized snot, there was wetness inside my nose when I inhaled.

A blizzard was coming.

Cocking my head, I listened. There was only Bonnie's snuffling breath and the whistling wind. After pulling off one of my work gloves, I scratched at my short beard.

"Losing my mind," I muttered.

When I glanced over my shoulder at where Toby had run off a minute before, he was tensed and staring into the distance. Was he chasing a hare like usual? The spotted mutt barked once sharply.

A baby wailed.

Heart thumping, I wheeled Bonnie with a nudge of my boot, urging her into a trot to follow Toby, who raced down a slope and up the other side. The terrain here was rocky, and I didn't push

Bonnie to go faster even though something was very wrong.

There was nothing down this way except a creek and old Coyote Trail. Yet as we came up over the rise, the cries grew louder, shriller, and absolutely undeniable.

That was a baby.

And the blot of red on the landscape sticking out like a sore thumb was a car.

I automatically reined in Bonnie. It was plain *wrong* to see a car on this land. But there it was—a small Ford, maybe? Cherry red and stopped at the side of the abandoned dirt road that everyone had called Coyote Trail. If I'd ever known why it had that name, I couldn't remember now.

The thin layer of snow showed the car's tire tracks. Even if it hadn't stopped here, it wouldn't have gotten much farther. The afternoon was growing darker by the minute. The sun set by four-thirty this time of year, and the approaching storm sure as shit wasn't helping.

Bonnie stamped her hooves, and I rubbed her tense neck. "Shh. I know. We're going home real soon."

Toby had stopped too, glancing anxiously between me and the car. There was a tall figure pacing on the other side of the vehicle, bouncing a bundle that had to be the crying baby.

Coyote Trail wasn't marked and had only ever

been known to locals—who also knew better than to try it now.

What damn fool would come down here with darkness and a storm closing in? With a *baby*?

I was mighty tempted to turn tail and leave him to it. I'd been looking forward to a quiet night by the fire with my book in one hand and petting Toby with the other. I sure as hell wasn't in the mood to deal with…whatever *this* was.

The baby screeched louder as if hearing my selfish thoughts, and I shifted in the saddle with a hot stab of prickly guilt. I'd never actually leave anyone stranded, let alone a child. Maybe they weren't stranded at all—though they would be soon if they didn't retreat back to the highway.

Nudging my heels and clucking my tongue, I got Bonnie moving. Toby raced ahead with a bark, and the man in the distance spun around and waved frantically. I lifted an arm in response.

The stranger—wearing a dark parka, a red woolen toque, and a gray scarf wrapped around the lower half of his face—hurried around the hatchback. "Thank God!"

He still held the crying baby, which was so bundled it was only a lump in a puffy yellow snowsuit and a thick blue scarf. Dark jeans clung to the guy's lean legs.

"What are you doing out here?" I asked, none too friendly.

"I was taking the shortcut into Lonely Creek." His low voice was muffled by his scarf, only his thick-lashed brown eyes visible between the scarf and hat. "Trying to beat this storm." Fat snowflakes began to fall on cue, and he looked up, those pretty eyes narrowed. "Might've made it if the engine hadn't conked out at the worst possible time."

"Nope. Rockslide cut off Coyote Trail." How did he even know it had existed? I added, "Maybe ten years back."

The man groaned. "Fuuu—" He was patting the squirming baby hidden against his chest through the layers of winter gear, and he glanced down at it. "*Fudge.* Do you have a signal? I don't have any bars."

I had to laugh. Heartily. "No service out here." My cell phone sat in a drawer except for when I went into town or Lethbridge.

He groaned again. "Look, I'm really sorry to put you out, but could you give us a lift to town?" He added, "Lonely Creek," as if there were anything else around. Aside from the ski resorts up in the mountains, Lonely Creek was it.

Staying upright with the baby, he bent his knees awkwardly to pet Toby, who nudged him enthusiastically, tail wagging. Toby hardly ever met new people.

"My truck's out by the big house," I said. In

only a minute, the snow was already falling more thickly, and the mountains had disappeared in a blink behind a curtain of white. "We've got to get inside."

I glanced in the direction of the two-lane highway, which was even farther and not busy at the best of times. It was way too far, and we'd have to flag down a passing vehicle. Even on a sunny summer day, it wouldn't be a great plan. It was a terrible one now, as much as I wanted to resolve this.

"You're positive the engine's toast?" I asked.

The guy nodded. "But I'm no expert, so please take a look if you can. The dealer promised this car had plenty of years left in it. It's only been a week."

He bounced the fussing baby as he walked back and forth, work boots crunching on the rocky side of the old road. Something about him seemed strangely familiar, but I pushed it aside. The clock was ticking.

I hopped down from Bonnie, who snorted disapprovingly but stayed put. Glad for my long leather duster as the wind whipped, I lifted the car's hood with a *creak* and peered inside. I knew a bit about engines—enough to know this one was beyond me even if I'd had tools in my saddlebag. I couldn't see anything glaring, so I closed the lid with a thud.

There was no other option. "We have to ride back to my cabin." I mentally said goodbye to my peaceful night. More than that, I hadn't had guests in…ever. Let alone a *baby*.

The man stared at Bonnie, who nosed at the ground. She was a tall sorrel horse, and though I wouldn't normally put two grown men on her back, we didn't have a choice. With darkness and snow closing in, it would take too long for me to ride back for my ATV. Besides, I trusted Bonnie's surefootedness more than the machine's.

Bonnie lifted her head, the fresh snow already blanketing her twitching ears, matching the white splotches on her face. I scratched her neck and murmured, "Sorry about this. It won't be for long." Louder, I asked the stranger, "Have you ridden before?"

The baby, who'd thankfully stopped screaming, gurgled unhappily. He patted her bundled back with his gloved hand and peered at Bonnie. "Yeah, years ago. But it's not safe for her."

"Bonnie's solid. She can handle the weight for a short distance." I glanced up at the gunmetal sky. We had to get the hell moving.

"I meant my daughter."

Oh. Right. I squinted at the yellow lump. I could understand not wanting to take a baby on a horse. "We'll go slowly, but we've got to go."

The stranger eyed Bonnie warily but nodded.

"What about all our stuff?"

"Just bring the necessities. The rest isn't going anywhere. No one comes down here."

"Okay. God, I'm such an idiot."

I wasn't about to argue, but I stayed silent and didn't pile on either. Neither of us could turn back time and change his terrible choice to leave the highway.

I paced while he put the baby into her car seat in the back of the hatchback—then pulled out bag after bag after bag. Christ, how did one tiny human need so much *stuff*?

I cleared my throat. "You're going to have to get that down to one bag."

"Um…" The man opened the jam-packed trunk area. He rooted around, coming out with a Toronto Blue Jays duffel. "If I put everything in here, does that work?"

"It'll have to." I removed Bonnie's saddlebag and saddle, keeping the bridle in place and feeding her a frosty apple from my pocket. "I'm going to leave these in your car."

He blinked at me. "We're going to ride without a saddle? Isn't that dangerous?"

"It's better for Bonnie. We can't both fit in the saddle, and if I ride behind it, it'll be a lot of weight on her kidneys." I squeezed it onto the driver's seat since it was the only empty space remaining in the car.

As I watched the guy shove diapers, bottles of formula, and jars of baby food into the Jays duffel, the earlier tug of recognition reared up and gave me a vicious kick. I sucked in a harsh breath.

Those thick-lashed brown eyes. Baseball. Long legs. Standing over six feet. Someone who knew old Coyote Trail existed.

No.

Impossible.

Hell no.

"Jake Gregson?" I accused, sharp as a blade.

Jerking upright from where he leaned into the back seat, he thumped his head on the rim of the doorway and yanked down his scarf.

This man wasn't a stranger after all. I knew the rotten core beneath that pretty face all too well.

Aside from facial scruff over his pale, smooth skin, the strong jaw and full mouth were the same. I hadn't let myself think about Jake Gregson in a long, long time, but face-to-face with him after— what, thirteen, fourteen years?—it all flooded back.

Desire. Idol worship. Betrayal. Shame. Fury. Hurt.

The hurt could still steal my breath after all this time, and I hated that more than I could stand. I also hated that the bastard was even hotter in his early thirties than he'd been as a teenager. And he was *here*, invading my land and my life.

I had no choice but to deal with it. I couldn't

abandon him and the baby to freeze. Where was the mother? The front passenger seat was stacked with boxes.

"Do I know you?" Jake asked. He peered closely at me. "I haven't been home in forever. Sorry, man. I'm blanking."

That shouldn't have twisted my guts. I shouldn't have cared. Of course he didn't remember. I'd been nothing to Jake Gregson. Never had been, never would be.

"Don't strain yourself." I kept my voice gruff and steady, because I'd let him know he could still hurt me over my dead, rotting corpse. "Cam Walsh."

He jerked like he'd been slapped before going very still. "Is that a joke? It's not funny."

I barked out a laugh. "Well, I *was* a joke to you. But no. I'm Cam Walsh."

Jake jutted his chin forward, cocoa eyes wide and jaw dropping. "*Cam?* But you were tiny." He waved his hand up and down to indicate my body. "And now you're—" He gaped.

I could admit I'd enjoyed reactions like this the rare times over the years that I'd run into someone from high school. Since my days were usually spent with Bonnie, Toby, and my yaks, it hadn't been often.

But I didn't puff up my broad chest and give him a wink like I had Madison Massey when she'd hit on me in the feed store in Lethbridge without recognizing me as the kid she and her friends had jeered at.

As I stared him down, Jake sputtered and shook his head. "Seriously? *Cam?*"

Then the weirdest thing in an already bizarre day happened: His face brightened with a smile.

He had no damn right.

But my stupid, stupid heart still stuttered in the face of Jake Gregson's gleaming teeth, the creases in his cheeks, and the crinkle of his eyes. Shit, the way I'd once treasured every single smile he'd granted me.

It'd been pathetic then. Now? My skin went hot with rage at my reaction.

The smile vanished as he snapped his mouth shut and swallowed thickly. "Um… Hey, man."

We stared at each other in silence, the snow falling thickly. Toby bounded to my side, looking between us with a confused little whine. In the back seat, the baby fussed with soft cries that would probably be screams again soon.

"Wow," Jake said, having the nerve to laugh. "You look so different. You're huge!"

I shrugged, trying to be nonchalant. "I was a late bloomer."

Jake had been the tall, buff guy back then. I couldn't get a good look at his muscles now under the parka, but at six-three, I was a couple of inches taller. It was a petty victory, but I'd take it.

"Ready?" I asked coldly.

"Um, I think so." Jake eased the baby from her car seat and examined Bonnie. "You're sure it's safe?"

Not answering, I grabbed the duffel and returned to Bonnie, taking hold of the reins. "You get up first."

"Right." Jake glanced around as if he was hoping for a last-minute save from anyone else. But it was just us for miles with snow and dark falling fast. "Wait, I'll get the carrier." He shifted the baby and awkwardly searched in the back seat with his barely free hand. "Can you take her for a sec?"

I didn't know shit about babies unless they were cows, yaks, horses, or goats. I dropped the crammed duffel and reluctantly reached for the squirming bundle. A delicate little face with big brown eyes peeked out from thick layers of wool and padding. She looked impossibly tiny to have that much lung power.

I'd once nursed the runt of Mrs. Pinter's goat litter, feeding him with a bottle and keeping him warm when he was abandoned. Animals were easy. This was a human, and humans were nothing if not complicated as hell.

"This is Cora." Jake was still holding on to her even though I had her securely under the arms of her snowsuit.

I said, "Uh-huh," because it seemed like he was waiting for me to respond.

He was still holding on. "I've got her," I said.

Frowning, Jake let go just long enough to yank out a harness thing before locking the door with an electronic beep. The car looked so old I was surprised it didn't require an actual key to lock.

As he strapped the harness to his chest, I held the baby uneasily. From under her toque and hood, she blinked at me with those huge, serious eyes, her thick lashes like her father's. I gingerly swung her back and forth. Babies liked motion, right?

Please don't cry again.

I breathed a sigh of relief when Jake took her back, buckling her securely against his chest facing him. Jake murmured, "We're okay. We're going to ride on a horsey! Yeah, we are." He glanced at me and dropped the light, singsong tone, his cheeks flushing red. "So, how do we…"

Dropping to one knee, I held out my gloved hands as a stirrup and ordered, "Put your boot in my hands. You're going to hold on to Bonnie's mane just before her withers." I glanced up to find him staring between me and Bonnie with an anxious frown.

Standing impatiently, I put his hand on the right spot before dropping back down. Jake still hesitated. I snapped, "Or you can freeze out here."

I braced for his weight. It was awkward with the baby strapped to him, but Jake raised himself over Bonnie, who obediently stayed still. I passed up the duffel, and Jake held it over his lap. "Scoot as far forward as you can," I said, before grasping Bonnie's mane myself. I reached behind Jake and over his thigh, brushing against him. "Brace yourself. I need to hold on to you."

I hadn't ridden bareback in ages. When I'd been a skinny kid, hopping up onto a horse had been a hell of a lot easier. I hesitated, glancing up at the darkening sky, snowflakes catching on my beard. We had to move, and I prayed I wouldn't end up flat on my face.

Bending my knees, I did a little skip-hop and threw my leg over Bonnie's back, holding her mane with one hand and gripping Jake's hip with the other as I pulled myself up behind. Bonnie remained steady, and I murmured, "Good girl," as I leaned around Jake to rub her neck.

There were no two ways about it: Jake was between my legs with my junk shoved against his ass. I had to reach an arm around him to control the reins. I let my left hand hang at my side, or else I'd practically be hugging him from behind.

Bonnie huffed, and I vowed to give her extra treats when we got back to the cabin. Toby was darting around, playing in the falling snow and having a grand old time as always. I urged Bonnie forward, and she picked her way up the slope and back to where the yaks grazed.

I tried very, very hard not to think about Jake Gregson's ass.

It was beyond bizarre to have him wedged against me, Jake sitting ramrod straight and stiff, one hand clutching the duffel on his lap and the other around the baby strapped to his chest. He smelled like sweat with a faint hint of…rose?

I could barely concentrate, my mind spinning, but Bonnie knew the way. We passed the yaks, who grunted and ignored Toby as he darted among them.

Jake said, "Those are weird-looking cows."

"That's because they're yaks. Humps. Horns. Shaggy coats."

"Oh. Right."

"Toby! Leave them be!" I called. Snow stung my face as the wind gusted. "Is the baby okay?"

Jake turned his head, bumping the brim of my Stetson. "Yeah. Sleeping somehow. She's magic like that."

I kept my eyes on the white horizon. His face was too close to mine, and I could hear the love in his voice. It made me remember a time when praise from Jake—even an offhand comment about how he liked my boots or something—had fueled me better than a Red Bull.

He added, "Thank you. Seriously, man. You

saved our lives." He sounded completely sincere, but he'd fooled me before. I said nothing.

Jake's breath puffed warmly over my cheek before he turned back. This had to be some messed-up dream. "Um, is it far?" He nodded to the fields in front of us, Bonnie walking at a good clip toward the cabin. She wanted back in the barn no doubt.

"A few klicks."

"What if the horse trips on something? If I fall off, I'll crush Cora." His voice was suddenly tight with worry.

I clenched my jaw at the insult to Bonnie, which wasn't really fair. I couldn't blame him— the baby was so tiny and helpless. After a moment of hesitation, I drew my left arm around, holding the reins in both hands, pressing fully against Jake.

"I won't let you fall," I muttered.

Jake tentatively leaned back against me, the bulk of his body against me pleasantly warm as the wind picked up. "Thanks."

Shit, it had been too long since I'd rubbed up against another man. If I was enjoying the feel of Jake Gregson of all people, I was clearly overdue for a trip into Lethbridge to have a few drinks and hook up with a convenient guy.

I realized as I thought back that it had been more than a year. Almost two, probably. I enjoyed getting off as much as the next person, but it had never been a priority the way it seemed to be for others.

As soon as the blizzard passed, I'd drive in for the night and find a guy. It would be a Christmas present to myself. I'd been working my ass off, and I deserved a break. First, I just needed to wait out the storm and get Jake on the road and back where he belonged.

I had no clue where that was—and I didn't much care as long as it was far, far away from me.

Chapter Two

JAKE

"*I WON'T LET you fall.*"

The sexy cowboy pressing close behind me was reassuringly strong and confident, and the horse under my already-aching butt did seem sure-footed.

The fact that said cowboy was somehow *Cam Walsh* blew my fuck—*flipping* mind.

I'd only cursed in my head, but I still peeked down at Cora guiltily even though she couldn't understand those words yet. Or any words.

Carefully, I lifted the scarf I'd wrapped loosely around her snowsuit hood, glimpsing her tiny face nestled close to my chest. She was still sleeping, her perfect bow-shaped pink lips parted.

I hated having her outside in this weather. On one hand, I was terrified I'd smother her if I wrapped her too tightly, but what if I didn't protect her well enough and she got frostbite? Her skin was so smooth and soft and *new*. I was probably doing everything wrong.

A stupendously stupid new item to add to my list of *Everything I'm Doing Wrong*: trying to take that shortcut. Such an epically dumb thing to do. Had I lived in Toronto so long that I'd forgotten just how isolated it was near Lonely Creek?

It was right there in the name for fuck's—*Pete's* sake. Nothing but ranches and cows around. And apparently yaks. Not to mention fierce blizzards that could kill adults, let alone innocent six-month-olds.

How did I think I could take care of a baby? How did I think I was even a little bit qualified to be a father?

Still, I *was* a father, whether I was qualified or not. I just had to fake it 'til I made it.

Any day now.

The horse whinnied and shook her head in the falling snow, and Cam leaned forward around me to pat her neck, murmuring, "Almost there."

With Cam's impossibly deep voice close to my ear, I held my breath. I hadn't been pressed so intimately against a man in years. Not since before Anna. And this man was *Cam*.

I'd wondered about him over the years. Of course I had. I'd never found a trace of him on social media, and I hadn't had the guts to ask any old friends what happened to him. If he'd landed on his feet after…

My stomach churned to think of it.

Well, apparently, he'd landed on a horse. And I was practically in his lap—just to make it even more awkward to see him again.

The snow blanketed the rocky land, accumulating rapidly, but the horse made her way steadily. I still couldn't see any signs of civilization, but Cam had mentioned a cabin. It was such a relief not to be alone that I hadn't questioned him. I wanted to ask for an ETA but bit my tongue.

Also, where exactly was the cabin? Did anyone else live there? Did Cam have a…significant other? Asshole kids had teased him in school and called him gay, but was he really? I had so many questions.

Fortunately, I had the sense to keep my mouth shut.

For the hundredth time, I cursed myself for thinking it was a good idea to take a shortcut. I should have stuck to the highway even if I'd ended up crawling along in the blizzard. But those huge trucks thundering along freaked me out, and I'd just wanted to get Cora home as quickly as possible.

Not that it was *home* anymore.

The snow fell steadily, gusting in the wind. If Cam hadn't found us…

I shuddered violently, holding Cora tighter before wincing and making sure I wasn't crushing her. My heart thudded as I checked her sleeping, peaceful face.

"What?"

I jolted again at Cam's question. More like a demand. "Just cold," I said. He grunted, and I could imagine he was thinking about how much colder I'd be if he hadn't found us. I tamped down another shudder.

I had to be smarter. I had to think of Cora and not take stupid risks. Not make impulsive decisions. I thought I'd learned that lesson years ago—especially after what I'd done to Cam. Yet here I was still making bad choices.

And here I was with *Cam*. I almost wriggled around to get another look at him under that Stetson to make sure I wasn't losing my mind.

"Here we are," Cam announced in that impressively gravelly voice. He'd been scrawny and pimply and so *young* when I'd seen him last. There'd been tears shining in his blue eyes that day—not to mention streaming down his red cheeks.

Again, I wanted to turn and examine his face, but I stayed put. Wait, where exactly were we? I squinted through the white. "I don't see anything?" Following a bark from the dog, I could barely made out a high-roofed wooden shack.

At least it had to be better than freezing to death in my hunk of junk car. I thought of Mary and Joseph finding no room at the inn. Did Bethlehem have blizzards like Alberta? Surely not...

I had to focus. My eyes stung as I squinted at the dark wooden structure. This couldn't be where Cam actually lived.

As if reading my mind, Cam said, "That's the barn. Cabin's to the right."

"Oh, cool." Though as the cabin came into focus through the snowfall, it was awfully small. Hey, it wasn't a barn! Mary and Joseph would have been jealous.

I wasn't particularly religious, but I prayed the blizzard would blow through and I could get back on the road first thing in the morning. Except the car was busted and would need a tow, and depending on how much snow fell, a tow truck wouldn't make it down Coyote Trail.

Fu—*fudge.*

The thought of asking Uncle Steve to pick us up filled me with icy dread. He was already doing us a huge favor. And there didn't seem to be a road here? Cam had said his truck was at the big house. That was *definitely* not here.

In front of the cabin, Cam hopped down from the horse more gracefully than a man that big had any right to. I tensed now that Cora and I were alone on the horse's back. What if it bolted and sent us flying?

But Cam had the reins, and the horse gave no indication she had any desire to carry us away to our doom. We just had to get down. No problem.

Except, why did the ground look so far away? With the snow, it was tough to make out where the ground actually *was*. We hadn't seemed so high with Cam solid and confident behind us.

Wordlessly, he grabbed the duffel and looped it over a broad shoulder. Who would've thought Cam would grow up into an actual cowboy? He'd been into horses and all that 4-H stuff, but when I'd imagined where he was now, I'd never pictured a taciturn rancher from an old movie.

I realized I was staring at the snow caught in his dark beard, boggling that he could grow facial hair at all, when he offered me a large hand. His lips pressed into a thin line. "Hold on and swing your left leg over toward me."

I did, grasping Cam's hand through the layers of our gloves, careful not to jostle Cora or whack the horse's head with my leg.

Sitting on the side of the horse, I asked, "What now?"

Muttering something under his breath, Cam grabbed me around the waist with both hands and plopped me on my feet in the snow as I swallowed a gasp. He stepped back quickly, looking like he'd love to wipe off his gloves as if they were covered in sh—*poop.*

He stalked toward the cabin, and I followed, ducking my head as the wind suddenly blew fiercely, snow swirling around us.

The air inside was cool, but compared to outside it was an incredible relief. Every cell in my body unclenched even though my butt and thighs were sore from the ride. Man, it really had been a long time since I'd been near a horse. I also hadn't realized just how cold I'd gotten. If we were still stuck out there…

My skin prickling, I breathed deeply, a faint scent of coffee and something spicy in the air. Cinnamon? I thought of my mom's cinnamon rolls, breathing through the wave of grief and wistful nostalgia.

I stood on the mat and eased down Cora's hood. She still slept, and I didn't move to unstrap her from my chest. I had a ton to learn about being a dad, but I'd figured out quickly to let sleeping babies lie.

Cam had brushed snow from his hat and duster and taken off his boots before kneeling by an iron wood-burning stove on the left wall. Sparks shot up as he pushed a log inside. I glanced around the cabin, which a real estate agent would optimistically call "*cozy.*"

Before the stove and small stone hearth was a

door through which I glimpsed a bathtub hung with a plain white shower curtain. Beyond the stove along the back wall were brown cupboards and a sink set in a beige laminate counter.

The fridge with microwave on top filled the right back corner with a double bed along the right wall. How did Cam even fit on that mattress?

The wooden bed frame had a simple headboard, and a window rattled faintly above it. A tall dresser sat in the corner to the right of the door, piled with battered paperbacks.

The wooden floor was covered by a couple of braided, multicolor throw rugs, and a rocking chair sat in the middle of the space facing the stove, a small table beside it. There was only the one chair, and it seemed clear Cam lived alone.

A simply framed photo of the Rockies hung near the fire, and there was another picture of what I now knew to be yaks on the wall beside the door. The fact that Cam spent long days with the herd and still had them decorating his cabin touched me for some reason.

I breathed deeply again, the smell of wood burning taking me back to camping as a kid. Sure, it was small, but the cabin *was* cozy.

"This is nice," I said.

Still wearing his cowboy hat and long leather coat, Cam rose and glared at me. He practically took up half the room. "I'm building a real house.

This cabin does the job in the meantime, even if it's not up to your standards."

"I wasn't being sarcastic! It really is nice. Homey." I tried for a joke. "Much better than a manger."

He stared blankly.

"You know, Mary and Joseph and Jesus. 'Away in a Manger' and all that? Not that I'm comparing Cora to Jesus. Just, you know. 'Tis the season. But I guess you're not a big holiday decorator?" There wasn't a single piece of tinsel to be seen.

He simply said, "No."

I cleared my throat. "I'm really grateful you're helping us. Thanks again."

Cam grumbled something under his breath, then peered uncertainly at Cora against my chest. "Does she…" He motioned with his hand. "Need anything?"

"Not right this minute. Formula and a diaper change soon."

Cam nodded. "As long as you know what you're doing."

I almost blurted, *Not even freaking close!* Instead, I asked, "Can I put her on the bed?"

Brow creasing, Cam glanced around. "Guess there's nowhere else. She won't fall off?"

"She's just starting to roll over. I'll watch her." I managed to toe off my boots on the mat, losing my left sock in the process, then eased her out of the carrier and unwrapped her from all the layers of insulation. I shrugged out of my coat, and Cam grudgingly hung it in the closet tucked behind the door.

Cora woke, her nose wrinkling as she debated between being upset or excited. Sitting on the side of Cam's bed, which felt incredibly intimate and wrong, I quickly lifted her high and blew a noisy kiss against her belly, the cotton onesie soft against my lips and nose.

I held my breath a moment, and…*there.* Cora cooed and smiled. The belly raspberry was my go-to for making her smile, which she'd just started doing in earnest. It made my heart sing every time.

After I placed Cora on the bed, she kicked and flailed her arms happily, making little contented noises that I could have listened to all day. I played the zipper game with my hoodie, pulling the zipper up and down in varying speeds to amuse her.

The floor was freezing under my bare foot, but the fire heated the cabin quickly. I kissed Cora's tiny hands, then her forehead. I inhaled deeply, that sweet scent of cornstarch baby powder and her special Cora smell grounding me. She was safe and happy, and nothing else mattered.

It was so quiet that I jolted when I glanced up to find Cam still looming on the stone hearth in his hat and coat, staring down at us with a frown.

He turned back to open the stove and jostle the logs with a poker before I could say anything.

Not that I had a clue what to say.

Cam Walsh! This hulking cowboy was *Cam*. I couldn't wrap my brain around it. What was he doing living out here all alone? Was that what he wanted? Was it my fault after what happened?

No, after what I *did*. It didn't simply happen. I did it. I made that horrible, selfish, scared, split-second choice.

I cleared my throat. "Cam, um, can I just say…" There were no adequate words, but I had to try.

"You need to call anyone?" He nodded to the ancient landline phone sitting on the dresser between book piles. It was the kind of phone with the buttons in the handset, a curved rectangle of beige plastic that sat in the receiver.

There was no modem in sight. No TV. Did Cam seriously not even have the internet? Even in the middle of nowhere, he could have had dial-up at the very least?

"Could I call my uncle?" I asked. "I don't want him to worry." Fat chance of that but I still had to let him know we were stuck.

Cam shrugged before tugging on his boots, opening the door, and disappearing into the snow. The door thudded shut behind him, the icy blast of air dissipating.

After checking the number on my cell, I picked up the phone, keeping one hand on Cora. Wow, I hadn't heard a dial tone since I was a little kid.

I punched in the number and braced as Uncle Steve answered with, "You there yet?"

Hello to you too. "Almost. The car broke down. Someone came along, and we're at his place now to wait out the snow."

Uncle Steve sighed. "You're not hurt?"

I was sadly grateful he'd asked. "No, we're both fine. We'll have to stay the night, though."

"You seen the news, boy? They're saying this could be a big one."

I groaned. "Sh—*oot*. Well, we're safe and warm, at least." I'd crammed all the formula and diapers into the duffel since they were the most vital, along with Cora's onesies. I could just wear the same clothes.

"You might be with this stranger more than a night."

My heart sank. A few nights with Cam in his cabin with one bed, assuming he wouldn't toss us out. Which I knew he wouldn't, despite his gruff talk. Well, awkward silence in close proximity to Cam was far preferable than the alternative.

I shuddered again, tasting acid as I imagined still being out there. The car would be buried in snow soon the way it was coming down. I rubbed

Cora's tummy, needing to feel her squirmy and warm under my hand.

"Who picked you up?" Uncle Steve asked.

"Cam Walsh. I knew him in high school, actually."

"Walsh? That queer kid?"

"No!" Not that I actually knew one way or another, but I instinctively wanted to defend him to Uncle Steve. Not that being queer should have warranted a defense, but with my uncle...

Uncle Steve grunted. "I thought he was raising yaks on a back corner of the Pinter place?"

"Oh, is that where we are? Yeah, I guess so."

Hal Pinter was one of Southern Alberta's most successful beef farmers, or had been when I left town. He owned a ton of land around Lonely Creek. The "big house" Cam had referred to must be Pinter's.

"How the hell did you get all the way out there?" Uncle Steve demanded.

Cringing, I admitted my mistake with Coyote Trail. As Uncle Steve grumbled about how I'd clearly been out east too long, I drew Cora closer, making her giggle and kick by tickling her cotton-covered feet.

Uncle Steve said, "You know we're spending the holidays with Janet's family up in Edmonton, so you'll have to figure out towing the car on your own. We got on the road this morning ahead of the storm."

I sucked in a breath. It made sense. How could I blame them? But it still hurt that they hadn't waited to say hi to me and meet Cora. Let alone invite us along in the first place so we could spend Cora's first Christmas with family.

I said, "Right, of course. I don't want to mess up your plans." I swore I could almost hear him thinking that I'd already royally screwed up his plans for my house.

No. Not *my* house. Uncle Steve owned it fair and square. It didn't matter that I'd grown up there. It was a rental property now.

In the silence, I added, "I'll take care of it. I just didn't want you to worry or anything."

"Yeah, okay." He sighed. "Carol's all right?"

"Cora. She's great. Thanks. Talk to you later."

As I returned the phone to its cradle, Cam stomped back into the cabin, Toby at his heels. I curled my bare left toes on the rug, shivering in the gust of cold air. Stone-faced, Cam kicked the door shut behind him, then took off his hat and coat, hanging them on the single hook by the door and leaving his boots on the mat.

Did Cam know how bad this storm was supposed to be? I wanted to say something, but I was afraid he'd bite my head off.

Wearing jeans and a plaid work shirt over a thermal, he crouched by the mat to brush snow off

Toby, who strained toward me excitedly but stayed put by the door until Cam gave him a pat on the rear. Nails tapping the wooden floor before being muffled by the rugs, Toby skidded over to me, his tail wagging violently.

Still sitting on the side of the bed with one hand on Cora, I petted him. He was brown and tan with spots—maybe part Collie? Hard to say. One of his floppy ears looked like it had been savagely torn, a great hunk of it missing. "Hey, boy," I murmured. "You're friendly."

In his thick green socks, Cam crossed to the kitchen area, switching on a hot plate sitting on the counter. He filled the kettle and put it on the burner. He asked grudgingly, "You want coffee?"

"That would be amazing. Thank you."

As I reminded myself yet again that awkward silence was much better than freezing to death, Cam made drip coffee with a plastic filter holder set over one mug and then another. He dragged the battered side table beside the rocker closer to the bed and thudded down a mug on it. "Here."

"Thanks." The coffee was strong and black, but I didn't ask for cream and sugar the way I normally would. I sipped what I could get gratefully, tickling Cora's kicking feet and giving myself a minute to breathe.

With Toby by his feet, Cam sat in the rocker, his stiff back to me. He could have been a statue.

His wide shoulders looked like granite, and there was no relaxed rocking. What did he do out here all alone without even a TV? Just *read*? Apparently.

The log in the stove popped and sizzled, and I wished we could turn on some random TV show to break the tension. I'd never wanted to watch one of the terrible twenty-four-hour news stations more.

I couldn't get over how *huge* Cam was. I'd been twice his size when we were teenagers. Cam had caught up and then some.

"This is wild," I said, needing to fill the silence. "I never would have thought…"

"What?" Cam snapped.

"When I imagined seeing you again, it wasn't like this." I thought of his splotchy red face that terrible day and opened my mouth to apologize, even though it was far too little and way, way too late.

Cam snorted. "That we can agree on. Look, we're stuck here tonight. We don't need to catch up or chitchat."

I had to do it. Rip off the Band-Aid. My mouth was dry, my pulse racing. "Can I just say—"

"*No.*"

He hadn't yelled. He'd gritted out the word like it was jammed in his throat. We both knew what I'd wanted to address. As much as I wanted to make things right—or at least tell him I truly was sorry—of course I'd respect Cam's wishes. I choked down the regret, a familiar action after all these years.

Cora screwed up her face, squeezing her brown eyes shut. That was her poop expression, and soon her full diaper would have her screaming. I gulped the fortifying coffee and reminded myself again that:

A) Awkward and/or angry silence was better than freezing to death.

B) It was likely only until morning.

I was determined to think positively. The media always blew snowstorms out of proportion these days. Everything was the "storm of the century," and then it would turn out just fine.

Still, it was going to be a hell—*heck* of a long night.

Chapter Three

CAM

THE BABY WASN'T crying, but she made noise almost nonstop. Gurgling, squeaking, grunting, and something that sounded a lot like laughing when Jake played with her. I hadn't thought babies that tiny laughed yet.

I could have asked Jake, but I didn't say a word. Sitting rigid with my feet flat on the floor, I stared at the orange glow through the ash-stained glass of the stove's door and gulped my coffee. Toby went back and forth between me and Jake, not sure what to make of any of this.

Join the club.

Normally, I'd have my legs stretched out and my feet propped on the stone hearth, Toby snoozing under my knees. My socks would get perfectly warm and defrost my toes while I sipped a spiked hot chocolate and read.

"Are those your feet? Yes, they are."

Jake's murmur behind me from the bed was gentle. Sweet, even. I could almost believe he really cared about the baby.

I scoffed to myself. 'Course he cared about her—she was his daughter. He wasn't a psychopath. A selfish piece of shit, yeah. But he seemed to be a good dad. Not that I knew anything about it.

I glanced over my shoulder. Jake was bent over the baby, tickling her. His brown hair still had a curl, the gentle waves tumbling over his forehead. He'd lost a sock in his boot, and I frowned at his bare toes on the rug.

The cabin had baseboard heaters that I only kept on in the bathroom since the stove heated the main area so well. Still, the floor was cold beyond the hearth.

The window rattled with a gust of wind. It needed fixing, but my new house was almost ready. The crew boss had told me I'd have the keys in time for the holidays, but they were already cutting it close, and this storm would put them behind schedule.

Not that it mattered where I spent Christmas. It was just another day. Either way, it wouldn't be long now until the house was done.

Too bad minutes were currently ticking by like hours. And…what the hell was that smell?

"Uh, Cam? Sorry to bug you. I need to change

her diaper. Do you have a garbage bag I can use?"

I got up to grab one from under the kitchen sink as Jake carried the baby into the bathroom. She started crying again, her little face going red. The bathroom was big enough for a tub with shower, a toilet, and sink.

I didn't know what else I needed, though the en suite in my new house was huge enough to live in. Mrs. Pinter had insisted that I'd regret it down the road when I got married, and I'd given in even though I knew the odds of me getting hitched were about the same as Toby learning French.

Jake took off his dark hoodie, revealing toned arms below his navy tee and the vulnerable bumps of his spine as he bent to put Cora on the tile floor with the hoodie cushioning her. The sole of Jake's bare foot was reddish—from the cold?

"Here." I grabbed a fresh towel from the rack. "Put her on this."

"It might get dirty. I have more stuff in the car but it wouldn't fit in the bag."

Squeezing beside him in the narrow space, I spread out the towel. "This is thicker than cotton."

"Thanks." Jake didn't look at me as he peeled down her baby outfit, unfastened the diaper, then—

I jerked back. "Jesus Christ!"

He chuckled. "I know. Amazing how a person that small can create...*that*."

I thought I'd seen it all when it came to shit and bodily fluids. I'd been shoulder-deep in cows and yaks struggling to give birth. It hadn't been pretty. But the foul stench and mess in that diaper packed a hell of a punch.

Shooing out a curious Toby, I stood back as Jake dumped the contents into the toilet. The baby squirmed, her cries inconsistent as Jake held up both of her little feet in one hand to clean her with a baby wipe.

The whole time, Jake talked to her in a sing-song at odds with his baritone, narrating what he was doing. He'd always had a deep voice that had made me—

Nope. Not thinking about that.

I watched him fit her with a fresh diaper. "How old is she?" My curiosity got the better of me even though I was breaking my own rules on keeping quiet. Why was I even still hovering over them in the bathroom?

"Just about six months."

I couldn't keep the surprise out of my voice. "She seems small."

"Yeah. She was in the NICU for nine days, and her adjusted age is twenty-one weeks. But her growth rate is normal. Her mother's petite, so the doctor says it's totally fine."

Here was a chance to ask about the mother, but I said nothing. It was none of my business, and there was no reason to give a shit. I wasn't sure what he meant by adjusted age, but it didn't matter.

As Jake wriggled the baby into a fresh outfit, he said, "Babies grow and develop at their own pace, and there's nothing to worry about."

He sounded like he had definitely been worried. More questions echoed in my head despite myself—exactly where was this mother, for starters—but I only stood there as Jake tightly rolled the diaper and wipe into a Ziploc, then bundled it in the garbage bag I'd given him.

Jake added, "She eats and goes to the bathroom normally. She's twelve pounds, two ounces now. I'm starting her on solid foods when we get to Lonely Creek."

Anxiety permeated every word. For a ridiculous moment, I wanted to reach out and clasp his shoulder. I only said, "Okay."

He laughed thinly. "I try not to obsess over percentiles and comparing her to other babies. But since my feed these days is all mommy influencers, it's hard."

It took me a second to understand what he meant by "feed." I hadn't had social media accounts in years. "Hm."

"Do you have a bucket or something?" he asked. "I'm not sure the best place to keep these."

Though the fetid odor had faded, it wasn't

gone. "Outside." I took the bag and sacrificed the mop bucket wedged under the sink. As I opened the front door, a blast of wind nearly knocked me back. Toby barked as though he could scare off the attacking storm.

Oppressive darkness and a mini snow tornado greeted me, and I tucked the bucket against the cabin wall beside the door. It was cold enough that the diaper would freeze before an animal could get at it. I had no idea how many diapers a baby went through a day, but it seemed smart to keep the bucket in arm's reach.

Toby still barked as I shouldered the door closed against the disturbing amount of snow falling. I bent to calm him, murmuring, "Thank you for protecting us from the weather."

The baby was mercifully quiet, and I returned to my rocker with my book, a dog-eared paperback thriller I'd picked up at the secondhand shop in town. The water ran in the bathroom sink, Jake still talking to the baby constantly.

My eyes danced over the same paragraph about ten times before I gave up and went to the chest of drawers. After cramming my socks in with my boxer briefs, I lined the empty drawer with a flannel blanket, folding it over for more padding.

When Jake emerged from the bathroom holding the now-calm baby against his lean, muscular chest, I said, "Here," motioning with the drawer still in my hands. "It's not a real cradle, but…" I put it on the bed since the side table didn't feel safe.

Jake smiled, and goddamn it, I hated the crinkles around his eyes. It wasn't fair that he should be so handsome. That he should be so gentle and loving with his daughter—whose giraffe-themed onesie was stupidly adorable—as he lowered her into the drawer.

Jake Gregson was a selfish POS. He wasn't supposed to coo and hum and smile adoringly.

Not that I wanted him to be a shit father. Why was I even watching Jake? Biting back a huff, I stalked to the refrigerator and poked around the freezer section. "Hungry?" I snapped.

"Uh, I'm fine. Thanks. I need to feed Cora soon." Jake zipped on his hoodie again. "I think I have a protein bar in my coat pocket."

The front door handle rattled, and I looked away from the selection of frozen dinners. Jake was bent over, examining the knob. Tight jeans stretched over his equally tight ass, which looked even better than it had in his baseball uniform in high school.

Irritated at myself for even looking, I demanded, "What are you doing?"

By the fire, Toby jumped to his feet, and Jake stood and whirled. "Sorry! I was just trying to lock it." He tentatively added, "I think it's broken. Just

FYI."

He was walking on eggshells, and if I was being fair—which admittedly I probably wasn't—I couldn't blame him. I laughed, though it was on the mocking side. "Lock? You've been in Toronto too long."

"Oh." His thick brows met. "But anyone could just walk in."

I laughed for real, and Toby resettled by the fire. "The yaks have no interest, don't worry."

Jake's face was still pinched, his gaze shooting to the baby sleeping in her makeshift cradle in the middle of the bed. Ah. I could—grudgingly—understand his concern.

"There really isn't anyone out here," I said. "The big house is twenty kilometers away, and the closest neighbors are more than an hour down the road past that."

Jake nodded and sat gingerly on the side of the bed, peering at his daughter, who tried to shove her tiny hand into her mouth. He exhaled a long breath before rubbing his face. His eyes were bleary and red, and I wondered when he'd slept last.

And why hadn't he put his damn sock back on? His foot had to be freezing.

When had he had a decent meal? If it was just Jake, I wouldn't give a shit. But he was apparently the only one around to take care of the baby.

"Butter chicken, General Tao, beef and broccoli, or red curry chicken," I said.

"You don't have to go to any trouble. Really."

I grumbled, "Just pick one."

"Uh…"

As the seconds ticked by, I added, "It's not life and death."

"Sorry. Whatever one you don't want."

"I bought them all because I like them." Why was he making this so difficult?

"Um, red curry? If that's okay?"

"Fine," I muttered.

"I need to heat up her bottle." Still sitting on the side of my bed with my down-filled plaid duvet wrinkling under him, Jake didn't move. The Jays duffel he'd pawed through for a diaper sat unzipped at his feet.

Though his eyes were open, for a second, I thought he might have actually fallen asleep. He sat there with shoulders hunched and that one sock missing, his expression blank. His remaining white sports sock didn't look warm enough for Alberta winter. He'd definitely been out east too long.

I closed the freezer door, and Jake jolted, mumbling to himself as he pulled out a container of formula and a bottle. While I microwaved the curry in its molded plastic container, he hesitated behind me by the sink.

"Is there a bowl I can use to warm her milk?"

Wordlessly, I rooted around for a plastic mixing bowl from the back of the cupboard and passed it to him. With his bare foot on top of the other, he ran the tap and filled the bowl with what I assumed was warm water, then stuck in the bottle.

I couldn't take it anymore. I went and grabbed a pair of red wool socks from the overstuffed drawer and tossed the ball at him. "*Here.*"

The socks hit Jake in the chest and dropped to the undoubtedly cold kitchen floor. He snatched them up and watched me uncertainly.

I sighed. Loudly. "Just put them on."

"Thanks." He pulled off his remaining sports sock and stuffed it in the duffel before tugging on my socks. His eyes crinkled, cheeks creasing with that wide, beautiful smile he'd always had. "Much better."

The microwave beeped, and I dumped the rice and curry onto a plate, giving it a stir before handing it over with a fork.

Leaning against the sink, Jake wolfed it down in record time. "Thanks. I needed that." He looked like he was about to lick the plate, but instead said, "I didn't take you for a floral china kind of guy."

My spine stiffened. "Didn't you?" I snatched back the plate and rinsed it under the tap. "The dishes are castoffs from Mrs. Pinter." Why was I explaining myself?

"I didn't mean—that's not…" Jake dropped his head. "I just meant it's…rustic out here. Sorry. Bad joke." He squeezed milk onto the back of his wrist the way they did in movies, then retreated to my bed to feed the baby.

In Jake's arms, she sucked enthusiastically with cute little squelching noises as he smiled down at her. Beyond them, the window over the bed rattled again.

I hadn't bothered with curtains since there were no neighbors. The window reflected Jake's head and the bathroom door, and I could make out snow gathering on the sill.

I wasn't hungry, but I forced down the butter chicken for something to do. Which was ridiculous given this was *my* cabin that had been invaded. The phone rang to temporarily rescue me from the awkward silence.

"Cam!" Mr. Pinter's voice boomed down the line.

"Hello, sir." I stood by the foot of the bed and shoved my free hand in my pocket.

I waited for him to launch into a complaint about a supplier or tell me again why the auction house wasn't giving him a fair deal. Or since he was traveling, he'd likely grumble about the airplane food. He'd always said I was a good listener when he needed an ear, and I did my best. It was the least I could do for him.

But tonight, Mr. Pinter said, "Is your pantry stocked, son?"

I blinked at the abrupt question. "Er, yes." I'd made a Costco run earlier in the week. Aside from one of the cupboards, my "pantry" was under my bed. I had cans of beans and soup and plenty of dried goods along with bread and microwave dinners in the freezer.

"Good, good. You heard the news?"

I went still. "No."

"How these fool weathermen didn't see something like this comin' down the pike, I'll never understand."

In the background, I could hear Mrs. Pinter say, "It's the climate change, Hal. The world's gone tush over teakettle."

I couldn't ignore the dread uncurling in my gut. "You need me to check on the herd or the big house?"

"No, Hal Jr. and his brood are there for the holidays to keep an eye on things just in case the staff need a hand."

I didn't say that the day Hal Pinter Jr. was remotely helpful would be a frosty one in hell.

"If I'd known this was comin,' I wouldn't have left," Mr. Pinter grumbled.

Mrs. Pinter harrumphed. "We're not missing

my sister's diamond anniversary. We're already in Barbados, and we are staying put."

"Yes, dear," Mr. Pinter muttered.

"I'm sure the storm'll pass," I said. "You know how those TV people are. Everything's an emergency."

"Mm. Though I have to admit, this one sounds different. Sorry I didn't call sooner, son. I know you're disconnected out there."

"Not a problem. I'm hunkering down with Toby."

I swore I could feel Jake's eyes on my back. Heat crawled up my neck. There was no sense in mentioning my unwelcome guests. There was nothing the Pinters could do about it.

I avoided crossing paths with Hal Jr., but it didn't matter one way or the other. The big house might as well have been the moon with the storm taking hold.

"Could get seventy centimeters," Mr. Pinter said. "They're probably closing the highway later tonight."

I bit back a curse. "Makes sense. It's really coming down."

"Could be blizzard conditions for days. Power will surely go, but your generator will keep the lights on. Did I tell you I got a hell of a deal on that?"

Mrs. Pinter called out, "Of course you told

him! We all had to hear about the generator for days! Now, you stay snug as a bug out there, Cameron! Merry Christmas!"

"Merry Christmas," I replied, smiling as I imagined her wrestling the phone from her husband and shooing him off to the beach.

I hung up, my smile vanishing as reality settled in. With that much snow and the wind blowing it, visibility would be nil. Jake Gregson wasn't going anywhere. Sure as hell not tonight, and not tomorrow without some kind of Christmas miracle.

I turned and surveyed my compact cabin.

And its one bed.

Chapter Four

JAKE

IT HAD GOTTEN dark so early that I couldn't believe it was barely eight p.m. It didn't help that I felt like I'd been up for days at an epic kegger—something I hadn't done for a decade. As I held Cora against my shoulder, encouraging a burp, my eyes were gritty and a dull headache throbbed. Fatherhood was a lot like being hungover.

Driving for days hadn't helped. And here I was, painfully—excruciatingly—close to our destination. Close, but so very far. I patted Cora's back as I paced the kitchen corner in Cam's warm socks.

Cam had settled into his rocker again, reading a book with Toby at his feet. Or at least pretending to read to avoid making small talk with me. He hadn't turned many pages.

As if proving me wrong, Cam asked, "Is she sleeping through the night yet?"

I laughed slightly hysterically. "I wish. She's getting better, though. For the first few months, she ate, and then she had to burp, which can take a while. She'd sleep for a couple of hours, and then it was time to heat up her bottle so she could eat again. And burp and poop, and sleep and eat and burp and poop."

"Jesus." He watched us with a furrowed brow. "That sounds exhausting."

"You could say that." I patted her back. "She's going for longer stretches now. It'll be amazing once she can get through the whole night. Some babies can at her age, but it just depends."

"And you've been doing all the driving coming out here?"

"Yeah, Cora's license got suspended. She's a speed demon."

For an amazing moment, Cam's lips quirked at my weak joke. "Why didn't you fly?" The question was barely out when Cam grimaced.

"It's okay," I automatically replied. It was, though. After the shit I'd pulled on Cam, I wouldn't expect him to have too much sympathy for me. "It's not that I'm afraid to fly. Not really. Intellectually, I know it's the safest way to travel. But I guess when your parents and three hundred other people plummet into the Pacific, it gives you pause." I tried to laugh it off.

Cam was looking at me with—yes, that was sympathy. I was pathetically grateful for it.

He said, "Especially with the baby."

My heart skipped. I hadn't even really put it into words, not even in my mind. But the thought of bringing Cora on board a plane and taking her up thousands of feet into the sky had been *unbearable*. I ran my hand over her wispy hair.

"Yeah," I managed, weirdly shaken.

"What?" Cam asked warily.

"Nothing." I gulped my second mug of coffee, which was lukewarm now and would only make me more jittery. I didn't say out loud that it was frightening to realize again how much I loved Cora. It was this instinctual, primal force inside me that I still wasn't used to.

I added, "Besides, we had to bring all her stuff. And as much of mine that I could squeeze in."

The plane crash had happened in my second year of university when I was barely twenty. It had left a hollow ache of grief that I'd learned to live with. Cora had softened its sharp edges more than I could have imagined. I would have done anything for my parents to meet her.

Cora finally burped. Swaying gently, I kissed her soft, perfect head and told her she was a good girl.

"Here," Cam said, standing. "Sit and rock her.

Babies like that, right?"

"Yeah, but we're fine."

"Just sit. I've got stuff to do." He opened the small closet by the front door and rooted around. Tail wagging, Toby joined him.

Honestly, I was so tired that I barely resisted a moan as I sank onto the chair. The wood was almost soft, and I relaxed gratefully, stretching my legs out, the hearthstone warm under my feet.

The wind howled outside, and I swallowed hard, trying again to forgive myself for that shortcut. I'd made plenty of mistakes, but that one could have been fatal. Cora depended on me for literally everything. How could I have been so stupid? So—

"Why *do* you have so much stuff with you?" Cam asked, his voice muffled by the closet, which he was apparently rearranging. "Seems like a lot for Christmas with your family."

"I don't really have family. I mean, my uncle's letting us stay in the basement unit of—" I had to stop and correct myself mentally before finishing, "—his rental property in town. I work remotely, so once my parental leave is over, it won't make a difference where I am. Rent in Toronto is just too much."

I waited for him to ask what I did for a living, but he didn't. Finally, I said, "I'm a customer success manager at a software company. Basically, glorified tech support for corporate clients. Solving their issues and keeping them happy."

Cam's response was a grunt. Then he said, "If your uncle's giving you a free place to live, that sounds like family."

"Oh, it's not free, but he's not charging the Airbnb rate, at least. There are barely any vacancies in Toronto, and the condo I was in wasn't rent controlled. The landlord tripled the price, and there's just no way. At least we can stay in Lonely Creek until I figure out where to go. But we're not close. Me and my uncle, I mean. Cora and I are an obligation to him and his wife."

In the silence, I added, "Still, I'm grateful." It sounded as hollow as it felt.

Toby wandered back, and as Cora fell asleep on my chest, I scratched Toby's head and rocked. Cam rooted around in the closet. My eyes grew heavy…

"Why come back here?"

I bolted awake at Cam's question. He was on his hands and knees in front of the closet, rearranging his shoes, which included three pairs of cowboy boots that all looked the same to me. Denim stretched over his meaty ass, and I marveled again that this was skinny little Cam.

While I'd realized in my second year of university that I appreciated male bodies just as much as female—or any gender—this was one man that I most definitely was not allowed to ogle. He'd taken us in, and it was beyond inappropriate. Aside from the fact that he hated me.

Though he seemed undeniably curious, which I took as a positive sign. I answered, "I guess it seems weird, huh? I had to move, and I dunno. I was searching apartment listings all over the country, but I kept thinking about home. Even though it's not really. My parents are gone, and like I said, I'm not close to my uncle and his family. I wanted to come back, though. I think it's the mountains."

I laughed too loudly at my own ridiculousness, and Cora whined and blinked. I nuzzled her head. "Shh. It's okay." She settled, and I exhaled. "Silly, right?" I whispered to Cam.

After a few moments of silence, he simply said, "No."

The chair creaked as I rocked slowly. "The air's so fresh here, you know? I figured it would be a good place to regroup. If I'm going to move us somewhere totally new, I need to research. Housing costs are up everywhere. Inflation is out of control. Now that I'm responsible for her, the stakes are so much higher. I don't want to screw up again. In the meantime... It felt right to bring her here."

After more silence, Cam asked, "What about her mother?"

I'd been waiting for this question and braced myself for a judgy reaction. "She's not in the picture."

People usually had a million nosy follow-up questions that hurt like hell—*heck* to answer, but Cam only said, "Okay," and I could have kissed him.

Whoa.

Where had that thought come from? I really was sleep deprived. I wasn't kissing anyone, let alone Cam Walsh. I couldn't even remember the last time I'd jerked off. I was too freaking tired. My life was dirty diapers and spit-up and formula. Not exactly sexy.

Shame filled me with a wave of nausea. Cora was the only thing that mattered. I shouldn't have been thinking about myself for even a second. I was irrelevant. The only thing that mattered was my baby. I was the only parent Cora had.

Resentment joined the guilt party as I wondered what Anna was doing now. Going out to dinner? Having cocktails with her friends at happy hour?

Then, warm and perfect against me, Cora made one of her adorable old-man grunts.

Everything else melted away.

Anna had made her choice, and I'd made mine. Cora was the best thing that had ever happened to me, and I didn't need Anna's help. I didn't need anyone's help.

Well, aside from my uncle's. My company topped up my salary to eighty percent during parental leave, but that missing twenty really left a dent. I'd bought the used Ford since we'd need a car in Lonely Creek, and look where that had gotten us.

I watched Cam polish his boots, buffing the leather with a stained rag. There were worse places to be.

After a few minutes of peaceful rocking, my curiosity won out. "What's the deal with the yaks?" I had many more questions, but I figured that was neutral enough.

Eyes on his boots, working the leather rhythmically, Cam said, "They come from the Himalayas."

Not really what I'd been asking, but I said, "Right. Do people eat them?"

"Yes. Organic lean meat that's juicy and high in Omega-3. Demand's growing every year. They're easier than cattle. Eat less, and they usually calve without issues."

"Cool." I closed my eyes. "Are they hard to handle?"

Warm with Cora against me and the fire sizzling nearby, I listened as Cam said something about…something…

Waking with a jolt of adrenaline, I immediately checked for Cora, who was fast asleep on my chest. I blinked at our surroundings, scanning for threats. The fire crackled beyond my feet in the dimness, the overhead light now off and a softer lamp glowing from somewhere behind me.

I couldn't see Cam, but I could hear him breathing. Presumably on the bed. Was he asleep?

I'd slept so deeply and suddenly that I'd barely even registered drifting off. I had no idea what time it was. If I sat forward or leaned to the side to glance behind me, I might wake Cora.

I softly cleared my dry throat, wishing I had thought to grab my water bottle. It was a rookie mistake to get settled with her and not have everything I might need within reach. And now my ankle was itchy. I slowly drew in my leg and strained to reach.

Behind me, Cam sighed. "Do you need something?" he asked quietly.

"Actually, water would be amazing."

The bed creaked as he got up. On the hearth, Toby lifted his head, then immediately went back to sleep. Cam still wore the plaid shirt and jeans, and I was disappointed not to see him in his PJs, which was ludicrous. For all I knew, he slept naked, which—

Which was *not* an avenue of thought I needed to pursue.

Cam passed me a cool glass of water, our fingers brushing before he let go. His skin was rough, undoubtedly from all the manual labor, and his hands were enormous.

Again, *not* what I needed to think about.

"Thanks," I whispered before gulping gratefully.

I realized it was the first time someone had been there to help me since I'd brought Cora home from the hospital. Just having Cam give me a glass of water felt monumental, and my throat clogged with sudden emotion.

Sh—*shoot*, I couldn't start *crying*. Even if I felt like a bag of ragged nerves barely held together with spit and duct tape, I had to get a grip.

"What time is it?" I asked too hoarsely.

Looming over us, Cam checked his watch, which was sturdy with lots of little knobs and was probably waterproof. "Twenty fifty-three."

Must have been a ranching thing to use the twenty-four-hour clock. "Oh. It felt like I was out for a while." It had only been twenty minutes at most. "Sorry, are we keeping you up? We can... Uh, I guess there's nowhere to get out of your hair."

Grunting, Cora woke and stretched. I held my breath, standing on the familiar precipice, praying she'd slip back under...

Not this time.

As she fussed, squirming and squawking, I

pushed to my feet, ready to begin the cycle again. There was a thin mattress on the floor in the space between the bed and the dresser with a blanket and pillow on top. Toby rubbed against my leg, and ugh, my ankle was still itchy.

"Is that for us? Thank you so much," I said. "I'll get her settled soon, I promise."

"I'll sleep on the bedroll."

While trying to soothe Cora, I shook my head. "You don't want me in your bed." Heat flushed my face as Cam watched me with an unreadable expression.

"I'm not letting the baby sleep on the god-damn floor."

"We'll be great, honestly! Cora has her make-shift cradle. Her manger."

"I'm taking the floor."

I wanted to argue again, but Cam seemed immovable.

An hour later, my eyes were heavy and my hands clumsy as I knelt on the bed and settled Cora in the drawer on the mattress next to the wall. I murmured to her as she fidgeted.

"Is it cool if I turn on my white noise app?" I asked Cam. "It helps her sleep."

"Fine."

I turned to find Cam in the bathroom door. He'd changed into flannel pajama bottoms and a white T-shirt that clung to his muscles. He still wore the green socks. The pajamas rode low on his hips, and I could see a sliver of flesh when he lifted one strong arm to flick off the bathroom light.

"Thanks!" I grabbed my phone and jabbed at the app, turning on the steady, soothing hum of the air conditioner option. I automatically checked my messages and email before remembering the lack of signal or Wi-Fi.

I realized Cam was still standing there watching. I asked, "Um, are you sure it's okay?"

"Huh? Yeah." He turned to the fire, then faced me with a huff of irritation. "What are you wearing to bed?"

It was on the tip of my tongue that I slept naked, but thankfully, I bit that back. "I can sleep in my clothes."

Muttering under his breath, Cam stalked to the dresser against the wall and yanked out a bundle of material before tossing it at me. I barely managed to catch it.

Wow, my hand-eye coordination was at an all-time low. My old baseball coach would have benched me in a heartbeat. Granted, I hadn't been this sleep deprived back in school.

"Thanks," I said, unfurling the soft flannel…onesie? I blinked at it. "Is that…Rudolph?"

Cam sighed heavily. "Yes. Pretty sure Dasher and Dancer and Prancer and whoever-the-hell are there too. It was a gift from Mrs. Pinter."

"Vixen."

His spine stiffened as his brow creased and tone sharpened. "Excuse me?"

"Huh?" I blinked back at him in confusion.

"What did you say about Mrs. Pinter?"

A laugh bubbled up. "No, the reindeer. Dasher, Dancer, Prancer, *Vixen*. Then Comet, Cupid, Donner, and Blitzen. I'm sure Mrs. Pinter is a lovely woman. Not that there's anything wrong with being a vixen." I yawned widely. What was I even saying? "Thanks for this." I held up the pajamas before unzipping my fly and tugging down my jeans.

Cam was suddenly by the fire, yanking open the door and shoving in another log in a shower of sparks.

I hesitated. Should I change in the bathroom? Was that weird? Would Cam take it as some sort of insult—like I was afraid to be naked in front of him because he was gay?

Was he gay? I honestly wasn't sure, and…

What was I thinking about? Changing. I needed to change. I paused. "Would it be okay for me to take a shower? Cora's sleeping."

Cam didn't answer.

Had he not heard me? Shit—*shoot*—had I not asked out loud? My eyes were so heavy. "Sorry. If that's weird, it's totally fine," I said.

Facing the fire, still prodding it with a poker,

Cam muttered, "It's not weird. Go ahead. Grab a towel from the bottom drawer."

"Thanks, man."

Under the glorious spray of hot water, all I could do was stand there and revel. For once, I didn't have to worry about Cora. Not that I was going to take hours, but I could enjoy a minute of peace.

After my minute was up, I washed quickly, hoping Cam didn't mind me borrowing his Costco shampoo and body wash. A white puff hung from the shower head, but obviously I didn't use it.

Stepping out of the shower, I shivered and grabbed the spare towel. The bathroom mirror was fogged, but the air still felt chilly. I rubbed myself dry and stepped into the onesie, zipping up the warm material. It was too big on me, but the flannel was cozy and soft on my skin.

Wait, should I have kept on my underwear? Was it weird to raw dog in Cam's pajamas? Shoulders tensing, I weighed the decision. I told myself it wasn't important, yet in that moment, it felt monumental.

My eyes burned, and I vowed I *would not cry over pajamas*. After a minute of deep breathing, I beat back the anxiety.

It was fine. Cam would wash the pajamas once Cora and I were gone, and—

Without warning, a wave of loneliness crashed

over me. Standing in Cam's bathroom in borrowed Christmas pajamas, I never wanted to leave.

I hadn't talked to any of my high school friends in years aside from the odd like or comment on social media. My university and work friends in Toronto didn't have kids yet, and I'd hardly seen anyone aside from a few perfunctory visits they'd made. My closest friends in recent years had been from Anna's circle, so they'd disappeared along with her.

It was fine. I had Cora, and I didn't need anyone else.

I crept out of the bathroom and tiptoed to the bed. In her makeshift cradle, Cora was fast asleep. I exhaled slowly.

Cam had the stove door open—still? Again?—and he crouched on the hearth and shoved another log inside. He was the first person I'd spent more than a few hours with since Cora's birth, not counting the NICU nurses. I watched him stoke the fire, so capable and strong, my loneliness receding.

Quickly followed by guilt that I'd be lonely at all when I had Cora. She couldn't talk, though. It felt good to be around another adult. Not that Cam was much of a conversationalist. Still, he could speak in words and sentences. Toby wandered over and licked my hand, tail wagging joyfully as I petted him.

"Turn off the light when you're ready," Cam said, nodding to the small reading lamp attached to the wall by the headboard. There was a small drawer built in under the lamp.

"Yep!" I answered far too cheerily.

Climbing under Cam's duvet wearing his Christmas pajamas felt incredibly intimate. He settled on the bedroll beyond my feet while Toby snuggled beside him. Cam spread his big hand over Toby's flank, petting him slowly. I tore my gaze back to Cora, who grunted in her sleep. I kissed one of her perfect hands before flipping off the lamp.

The fire lit the room just enough that I wasn't in blackness. The wind howled fiercely, and I prayed the odd rattles of the window wouldn't wake Cora. I curled on my side, listening to her burbles beyond the drone of the white noise. Hopefully, I could get a few hours before she woke…

It was still dark when I opened my eyes again. I reached gently into the cradle—and panic exploded as I bolted up, tumbling out of bed to my feet, spinning around, my bleary eyes searching the unfamiliar shadows. I nearly tripped over Toby, who was instantly alert, barking once.

His deep voice somehow still commanding, Cam whispered, "Toby, shh!" from the rocking chair.

Where he cradled Cora in his huge arms.

Chapter Five

CAM

A S JAKE SPUN and stumbled, his hair a bed-head mess and his brain clearly still half-asleep, I nodded at Toby, who'd curled again on the rug. "Good."

Jake blinked down at Toby near his feet as if he didn't recognize him. Beside the chair, he bent over me and palmed the baby's head, peering at her intently.

Firelight flickered on his face so close to mine, his long eyelashes illuminated. The white noise still droned from his phone on the bed, or I could have heard the whisper of his breath. Was that the tickle on my cheek?

This is Jake Gregson. Stop it.

The sooner he could get the hell out and disappear back to his own life and leave me to mine, the better. But snow still fell, the wind still whipped, and we were stuck together. So, there was no reason I couldn't keep holding the baby since she'd settled. It wasn't her fault her father was an asshole.

Though right now, wearing my reindeer PJs and wiping sleep from his eyes, he didn't seem like an asshole. He seemed almost as vulnerable as the baby.

I murmured, "She's fine. You were dead to the world, and I didn't want to leave her fussing."

Jake knelt, still gazing at his daughter as if she was the most precious thing in the universe—which I supposed she was. He rested a hand on the arm of the chair, his ribs brushing my knee where he leaned close.

"Do you want to…?" I lifted my arms, the baby hardly weighing a thing.

"No, no. Don't disturb her," he whispered. His brown eyes focused on me. "Unless you want me to take her? I'm sorry. You should have woken me."

I lowered her, the baby still asleep and warm, her eyes flickering and tiny pink lips opening once in a while. "I was already awake."

"What time is it?" Jake rubbed his face and stood.

"Probably five-thirty or so by now."

The white noise stopped, and in the sudden silence, my heart was thudding too loudly.

Jake dropped down at my feet, gazing at her with wonder. "Whoa. She slept through the night. Or close enough."

"Guess you both needed it."

"I'm so proud of you, Cora." He beamed at her.

"Cora," I repeated. "Suits her."

Jake's smile dimmed but didn't fade completely. "It was my mom's name. Felt right."

I wasn't sure what to say, so I kept my trap shut. Why was I even talking to him? I needed to hand over Cora and go back to ignoring them as much as possible. But on cue, she hiccupped and lifted her tiny, wrinkled hands before quieting.

How was I supposed to ignore how damn cute she was?

"I can't believe I didn't wake up." Jake rubbed his face again, his stubble scratching. "If you hadn't been here…"

"You would have woken eventually."

Staring at the ceiling, I'd waited for Jake to soothe the baby when she'd started whimpering and complaining. The seconds had felt like hours. It would only have been a matter of time before she'd started full-lunged crying, and Jake was so deeply asleep that I'd acted automatically.

Not that I gave a shit about Jake.

There was just no point in standing there with my thumbs up my ass waiting for the baby to wake him. It had seemed impossible that he didn't even stir when I'd leaned over to pick her up from the drawer, but he'd clearly needed the sleep after driving for days.

It turned out human babies weren't so different from newborn goats. I'd warmed up a little formula since I figured it would calm her. She'd stopped crying almost immediately when I'd held her and had suckled happily on the bottle in my arms as we'd rocked.

I'd burped her, bracing for spit-up, which I'd only seen in movies. But she'd only let out air before settling again in my arms. I wasn't eager to change a diaper, so I'd figured she'd be fine until she wasn't.

Cora was *so* incredibly small. I'd been afraid I'd break her, but she'd babbled contentedly. She was doing it again now, and I couldn't help but smile. I glanced at Jake—to find his eyes on me instead of his daughter.

He jumped up, grabbing the bottle from where I'd left it beside the chair, soon washing it in the sink by the light of the fire. Toby was snoozing again—he slept at the drop of a hat—and my chair creaked as I rocked slowly. Toby would need to go out soon, but he could wait for the moment.

Cora was gurgling and groaning, and I asked Jake, "Is that normal?"

He chuckled from the sink, where he was mechanically drying the bottle with the Newfoundland tea towel Mrs. Pinter had brought me back last year. "Yep. Babies make so much noise. I had no idea." He scoffed. "That's the tip of the stuff-I-didn't-know-about-babies iceberg."

"You seem to know a lot," I said before I could remind myself yet again that I wasn't supposed to be talking to Jake.

"Fake it 'til you make it. It's just me, so I've got to figure it all out."

I didn't want to ask. It was none of my business, and, again, *I wasn't supposed to be talking to Jake.* I'd taken him in because he and Cora would be dead if I hadn't, and—

I shivered, holding Cora a little closer. If she hadn't cried, I never would have gone over to Coyote Trail to investigate, and they'd still be there trapped in the car with no heat. They'd genuinely be dead or close to it by now, and the thought had acid swirling in my gut. I didn't have to like Jake to be glad he and Cora were safe.

I traced the delicate shell of her ear, grateful for her lung power. And Christ almighty, I had to know. I asked, "What happened to Cora's mother?"

The firelight cast shadows over Jake's stony face. "Nothing," he replied flatly, still clutching the tea towel. "She's not dead or anything. She didn't want Cora. Or me either, it turns out."

"Then why did she have a baby?"

Jake ran the tap and washed the clean bottle again, scrubbing the lid. "It was her choice. I told her I'd support whatever she wanted to do. I guess Catholic guilt set in, and she decided to carry Cora. She arranged for adoption—or should I say her boyfriend did."

I frowned. Cora squirmed, and I gave her my pinky finger to suckle. She did, her soft lips wet on my fingertip. "You weren't her boyfriend?"

Jake laughed hollowly. "I was, actually. For seven years. Unbeknownst to me, she and her boss started an affair a few years ago. He promised to leave his wife—every cliché in the book. But then he actually did, and Anna left me. I came home from the gym one Saturday morning, and she was gone. Must've really busted her ass to clear out almost all her stuff while I was doing leg day."

I said nothing, waiting. Trying not to imagine how painful that must have been for him.

Screwing and unscrewing the bottle lid, Jake went on. "She left an apologetic note, but she wrote it quickly. I could tell from the way she hadn't made her usual neat little hooks on the ys and js. Then, a few weeks later she shows up at our—*the*—condo red-eyed and pregnant. Turns out the boss man doesn't want more kids. And Anna's never wanted them either."

"You're sure Cora's..." I couldn't resist asking.

"Yep. Did a paternity test before she was born. Anna insisted on it. Anyway, I told Anna it was her choice, which obviously it was. I'd thought about having kids one day, but it wasn't, like, a lifelong dream or something. It was a maybe, somewhere on the horizon. I was fine with Anna not wanting to be a mother. I figured it would all work itself out one way or another." He laughed sharply. "I guess I was right about that."

In my arms, Cora burbled and groaned and opened her eyes. Jake apparently recognized her waking sounds, since he was suddenly there to lift her up and murmur a sweet good morning to her. In the ridiculous reindeer onesie, he bounced her gently, pacing by the hearth.

Toby whined, woofing softly, which I knew meant it was bathroom time. I had more questions—especially why Jake had kept Cora instead of going through with the adoption—but the blast of frigid wind when I opened the door to let out Toby broke the spell.

I ordered him to stay close, and he did, racing back to the door in record time. As much as he loved snow, Toby clearly recognized this storm wasn't to be underestimated.

I had to dress and check on Bonnie in the barn, but I couldn't remember the last time I'd seen a snow squall this bad. It was a total whiteout, so I'd have to wait at least until the sun was up. I flipped on the lights while Jake took Cora into the bathroom.

In the light of the fire, with Cora warm and sweet in my arms, talking to Jake had felt right in a way I couldn't explain. Now, I could refocus. As soon as the storm passed, I'd take Jake and Cora to Lonely Creek, and I could get back to my routine. This would be nothing but a blip on the horizon that I'd forget in no time.

THE STORM HAD no intention of passing anytime soon.

With the high winds bringing whiteout conditions, my trip to the barn to check on Bonnie was short. On my way back, I couldn't see anything but snow, and I had to stop for a minute and wait for the wind to shift. It blasted my face, and I closed my watering eyes against the sting.

It was frighteningly easy to get turned around in a blizzard like this without any landmarks. I knew the cabin was ahead of me. Normally, I'd be able to see it clear as day. On my way to the barn, I'd been able to make out the dark wood angles of the barn roof.

Now, when I looked behind, the barn had vanished like it had never been there at all. Fortunately, the wind shifted direction just enough for me to spot the shadow of the cabin. I hurried onward, the familiar, comforting shape of it getting clearer. As much as I wanted a real house, I'd miss my cabin when the time came to move.

There'd be no work done on the house until the storm passed, and then it would be Christmas and Boxing Day. Maybe it would be finished by New Year's if I was lucky.

I grabbed firewood from the box that sat against the cabin wall, knocking off at least a foot of snow from the lid. Inside, I left the wood on the mat while I took off my boots and coat before stacking the chopped logs in the black iron rack by the stove. One jagged piece of wood caught on the wool of my sweater, and I tugged impatiently.

Returning to the mat, I yanked off my work gloves and placed them in their bin in the closet. With a thud, two of the logs I'd stacked tumbled to the hearth. Toby jumped up, barking and eyeing the firewood suspiciously.

"Thank you for protecting us from the inanimate objects," I said, ruffling his head before bending to pick up the logs—and getting a sliver jammed into my palm. "Son of a bitch," I muttered, wincing.

"You okay?" Jake asked. He was still wearing the reindeer pajamas and had no right looking so good in clothing that silly.

Heat flushing my cheeks, I pointedly didn't

look at him now in the rocker. "Fine."

Under the bathroom's bright bulbs above the mirror, I inspected my hand. I'd done a good job of it, and of course the splinter was in my dominant right hand. Grasping the tweezers with my left fingers, I poked uselessly, muttering under my breath.

"Are you sure you're okay?" Jake asked tentatively from the other room.

"*Fine*," I repeated. Not that being stubborn was getting me very far. My fingers felt clumsy as I tried to grasp the annoyingly tiny end of the substantial sliver. I dropped the tweezers into the sink.

In the mirror, Jake appeared behind me in the doorway. "Do you want me to…?"

Sighing, I handed over the tweezers and stuck out my palm. Jake took my hand, his fingers warm. Concentrating, he bent his head, prodding at the wound gently. His exhalations tickled my palm, and in the mirror, I could see thick-lashed eyes focused seriously. There was no trace of the cocky star pitcher he'd been in high school.

I almost snapped at him to just yank it out already. Instead, I grumbled, "It's not a big deal."

Not looking up, Jake murmured, "It's getting red. Could become infected. Just hold still."

His warm grasp on my hand, and the whisper of his breath on my skin, and the scent of his shampoo—of *my* shampoo—in his thick, wavy hair were too much. We were standing way too close. I could have bent and rubbed my cheek over his head…

Brow furrowing, Jake straightened. "Am I hurting you?"

My heart thundered, face flaming as I tore my gaze from his. How were his eyelashes so long? And those freckles on the tops of his cheeks were ridiculous. *And* he was still cradling my hand in his so gently, as if I were the baby.

Why didn't I hate it?

Why couldn't I still hate him? After all these years, I'd let him get to me in less than twenty-four hours.

Pathetic.

"No," I managed, the word scraped from my dry throat.

He still frowned at me. "Sorry. But it has to come out. Hold still." He bent his head again.

I couldn't move a muscle, so he didn't need to worry about that. I was frozen in place like one of my yaks with a hoof stuck between rocks. My eyes cut to the mirror, watching Jake.

He bit his lip as he pushed at the wood embedded in my flesh, trying to get another millimeter free to grasp with the tweezers. I watched where his tooth dug into the meat of his bottom lip, and I wondered what it would feel like to lick across that lip…

"Got it," Jake whispered, sending goosebumps up my arm. "Easy does it…"

Slowly, slowly, he freed the sliver, which was narrow but long. I exhaled as Jake lifted his head, his face creasing into a smile. The faint discoloration on his lip where he'd bitten flushed back to red. He was still holding my hand, and all I could do was stare at him, unmoving.

Jake's smile faded, and his Adam's apple bobbed as he swallowed hard. His gaze dipped to my mouth and back to my eyes, and his own eyes flared dark—which made no sense, because there was no way in hell Jake Gregson was thinking about kissing me. He was straight.

Besides, I didn't want to kiss him! He wasn't allowed to crash back into my life and be so damn *likable*.

So damn *kissable*.

Then why couldn't I stop thinking about his mouth?

Toby's confused whine from the doorway jolted me and Jake, and he dropped my hand, fumbling with the tweezers, which bounced on the counter with a metallic clatter.

"There you go! You should disinfect. Do you have a first aid kit? I can…" He was backing up, though.

"I've got it. Thanks."

"Great. It's tummy time."

I blinked at him, my brain trying to figure out what the hell he meant. Was that some kind of insult? I didn't have rock-hard abs or anything but—

"For Cora," he added. "It's a thing for babies. Tummy time? It helps their development, and—" He shook his head. "Doesn't matter. I'm just going to do that." He vanished into the main room.

I welcomed the sting as I disinfected the tiny wound. This storm had to pass soon, and my life could go back to normal. Me, Toby, Bonnie, and my yaks. I'd have my new house to move into any day now when the weather cleared.

I'd worked for years to afford it, and so what if it would be a little big just for me and Toby? I didn't need anyone else. And even if I did, it wouldn't be Jake.

Chapter Six

JAKE

O N HER BELLY in the middle of the mattress, Cora kicked and pushed up with her hands, grunting and grimacing.

"Good up-dog!" I said from where I knelt at the end of the bed.

She whined, ready to cry at any moment. She wasn't in the mood for tummy time, and frankly, neither was I.

"Hey, um, do you have a shaving mirror?" I asked Cam.

He was in the kitchen—reorganizing a drawer?—and he silently disappeared into the bathroom, returning with the round mirror. Over jeans that hugged his thick thighs, he wore a cream, cable-knit sweater that made me think of Chris Evans in that whodunit movie.

"Thank you." I smiled as I took the mirror,

but Cam's dour expression didn't flicker. Keeping my voice cheery, I slid the mirror in front of Cora. "Look who it is!"

But she still whined, her reflection not entrancing her today. I sighed and mumbled, "Come on."

Cam was back in the kitchen. He said, "Why are you doing that if she doesn't like it?"

"It's important for her development. If babies spend too much time on their backs, they can get flat head syndrome. They have to sleep on their backs, so we try to get them on their stomachs as much as possible."

We. I almost snorted. I was talking like a parenting pamphlet, which were all, we this, and we that. It was me, myself, and I running this show.

Toby licked my face, and I laughed, pushing at his muzzle. "Thank you for your support." He wagged his tail and licked my hand. Once Cora and I were settled, I'd have to weigh the extra expense and responsibility against the comfort of having a dog.

I let Toby lick away at the back of my hand and asked Cam, "Where'd you get him?"

"He got me. I was working out on the south paddock on Mr. Pinter's herd. Toby showed up and spooked the cows. He only wanted to play. Hal Jr.—" Cam broke off. His back was to me as he emptied a drawer onto the counter.

"Mr. Pinter's son?" I prompted after another beat of silence.

"Mm-hm. He was in town. Thought Toby was a coyote. Toby was scrawny, but any fool could see he was a dog."

"Is Hal Jr. a special kind of fool?"

Cam made a huffing sound, and my heart lifted as I realized it was a reluctant laugh. "He is."

As I turned the mirror this way and that, trying to keep Cora engaged as she kicked, I asked, "He didn't want to be a rancher?"

"He's an 'entrepreneur.'"

The disdain dripped from the word, and I chuckled. "Who still imagines himself as a rancher too? Let me guess: Did he move to Calgary?"

Cam sounded surprised. "Yep."

"I haven't been in Toronto *that* long. I remember the type." I petted Toby with one hand, squirming my face away to avoid more kisses, and shifted the mirror for Cora. "I'm glad Toby found you."

"Me too. Hal Jr. was going to shoot him."

I jerked. "Fu—*dge*. Good thing you were there. Poor Toby." I stroked his head, letting him lick my ear. "I bet Hal felt like a fool when he realized it was a stray dog."

"He would've been happy to shoot us both."

"Whoa. That's dark."

Cora pushed higher with her hands, and I

smiled and encouraged her. One of the weird things about being a parent was having serious conversations or watching awful things on the news while simultaneously making big happy faces for Cora.

"He wouldn't really," Cam said. "He's many things, but he's not evil."

"Just petty and stupid?" I gasped playfully for Cora and mumbled, "Big push!"

Cam grunted assent.

"He didn't want to stay and take over the ranch from his dad?"

"Not the day to day. He'll inherit, along with his sister in Edmonton. He's got lots of grand plans, but he doesn't like getting his hands dirty."

My hands were still full with Toby and Cora. My knees were getting sore, but I didn't want to disrupt Cora's flow now that she'd focused on the mirror. I squirmed as Toby licked my ear again.

"How will it affect you when Hal Jr. takes over one day?" I asked.

Cam grunted again. "It'll be a pain in my ass."

I waited for more, then prompted, "Could he kick out you and the yaks?"

"I bought this land fair and square from Mr. Pinter. I'll own the road to my new house too. Mr. Pinter made sure of that. Still have years of payments to make to the bank, but it's mine."

"That's amazing. Mr. Pinter sounds like a great

guy." I made a surprised face for Cora. "How did you end up working for him?"

Cam was quiet for so long that I wasn't sure he'd heard me. Then he said, "My dad was his foreman. When he had the heart attack, Mr. Pinter drove him to the hospital himself while one of the ranch hands did CPR in the back. It was no use, but they tried."

That rang a faint bell, and I cursed myself for not remembering. "I'm sorry. So, he gave you a job?"

Another long silence. Cam stood like a statue in the kitchen, his back to me. Unease crept down my spine.

Finally, Cam said flatly, "He was the only one that would. After I was arrested, U of A took back my admissions offer."

That hit like a freight train, and I pushed to my feet with a surge of adrenaline—quickly followed by horror and shame. I should have known all of that, but I'd escaped to Toronto, my scholarship to U of T intact since I hadn't been arrested.

I was breathing heavily, and I shook my head as if I could make it untrue. "Cam, I…" I could barely look at him—though his back was still to me. Then I glanced down and gasped.

Standing there in Cam's reindeer onesie, with regret filling me to bursting, I watched Cora roll over onto her back for the very first time.

As Toby barked once uncertainly, I exclaimed, "Oh my god!" Joy elbowed in, and my eyes burned with the mess of emotions.

"What?" Cam was there in two strides, peering down at Cora with concern.

"She rolled over. She rolled over!"

I'd grabbed his arm without thinking, the muscles warm and solid beneath wool. It was such a thrill to have someone there to share the moment with. I wanted to throw my arms around him and whoop, but caught myself.

My eyes burned as I scooped up Cora. "I'm so proud of you, sweetie." I kissed her soft cheeks. "She did it all on her own! I was hoping she would soon, but you never know," I babbled to Cam before placing her back on her tummy on the bed.

He looked down at her, a whisper of a smile softening his expression.

I crouched. "Can you do it again, Cora? Come on, show Cam."

It was probably ridiculous, but I wanted him to see her roll over so badly. I almost forgot who it was and where we were, but as we stared at Cora kicking on her stomach, Cam standing awkwardly, I remembered.

I forced a laugh. "I mean, she's not a dog. Sorry. I'm sure you have better things to do." Toby tried to lick my face again, and Cam returned to the kitchen, beckoning Toby to follow. He reached for a bag of dog treats, making Toby sit before giving him one.

Standing at the sink, Cam said gruffly, "That's good that she rolled over."

"Yeah." My face burned. He probably thought I was being ridiculous. "Thanks. The perfect Christmas present. I'd wanted to get a tree and decorate for her. Wrap presents that she can't really open yet. Stupid, I know. She's too young. But it's still her first Christmas."

"It's not stupid."

"Thanks."

There was so much more I wanted to say— needed—to say, but the air felt thick. And before I knew it, Cora's poop face was back.

The day ticked by. The power went out, but Cam had a generator. The phone line was dead too, so we were well and truly cut off from the world. Not that Uncle Steve was going to be calling to check on me and Cora.

I slept when Cora did, curled up in Cam's bed. I swore I could feel his eyes on me, but it was surely only my overactive imagination. Aside from talking to Toby occasionally, Cam and I had lapsed into a fraught silence.

Or at least it was silent until Cora started crying.

"I'm sorry," I said again, bouncing her in my

arms as I rubbed her back. Her wails didn't subside, and I desperately tried the bottle again. It'd been over an hour of her crying, and the cabin was so small, and the fire in the stove so hot. I tugged at the neck of the onesie.

Sitting in his rocker, still wearing the sexy sweater over jeans, Cam muttered, "Babies cry. It's fine."

"Yeah, but there's usually a reason." I urged her to drink, but she flailed her arms, red-faced as she screeched. "Okay, you're not hungry," I mumbled.

I checked her diaper again. Dry.

"Come on." I was close to whining. "*Please.* What's the matter, sweetie?"

She'd been great earlier. She'd *rolled over*! That victory seemed a million miles away. Cora's piercing wails only intensified, making me cringe.

I paced the tiny kitchen as Toby started barking. A building headache stabbed behind my eyes. What I wouldn't have given to go back to the awkward silence that had permeated between me and Cam all day. I'd take *any* kind of silence.

Cam's book was still open, but there was no way he could concentrate to read. It was getting dark again in the late afternoon, the white outside the window dimming.

"Toby!" Cam snapped his fingers, and Toby stopped barking, though he still peered at me and

Cora uncertainly.

"I'm sorry," I repeated.

Cam shook his head. "Dogs bark. Babies cry. Just like we talk."

"Well, she talks a lot more than you." I said it without thinking.

His jaw tightened. "What do you want me to say?"

I rubbed my face. "I don't know. Whatever you want. Or not, in your case. I guess you never were a big talker. Except when baseball cards came up." I glanced around, eager for the distraction. "Do you still collect them?"

"No," he replied stonily.

His tone made me think it had something to do with me. As Cora wailed, my chest tightened with a punch of guilt. He'd loved baseball and baseball cards. Sure, I'd been the star pitcher on our school's team, but it was small-town Alberta. I'd never been destined for the major league—or even the minor. Had I ruined the whole sport for him?

Eyes screwed up, face red, Cora kicked and screamed. "Shh, shh. It's okay." I paced between the fridge and the sink and suddenly stumbled over Toby. My heart lurched as I gasped and righted myself, squeezing Cora tighter. Tail wagging, Toby circled us.

"Toby!" Cam leapt up, the chair rocking back

and forth violently in his wake. "Enough." He ushered Toby into the bathroom and shut the door. He didn't slam it, but the air still felt thick.

"We're fine," I said, placing Cora in the drawer atop the bed. I sat on the side of the mattress and put a hand on her tummy. "You want to sleep again? Here you go." I wanted to beg, "*For the love of all things holy, go to sleep!*"

She kicked her feet, screeching.

As I rummaged in the duffel, trying not to panic and failing miserably, Cam loomed on the hearth, hands on hips. He asked, "Does she do this a lot?"

My heart thumped. "Not like this." My fingers searched the bottom of the duffel. "It's in the car," I mumbled. "Do you have a thermometer?" It wouldn't be the in-the-ear kind I had, but anything would do.

"She's sick?" He stepped closer, frowning.

"I don't know!" I hadn't meant to shout. I swallowed hard, pressing my hand to her forehead. Toby barked in the bathroom, and Cora screamed, and I wanted to jam my fingers in my ears.

"Does she feel warm?" I asked, which stupid since I was the one touching her forehead. Her skin was flushed, but was it from a fever or working herself up into a state over something I couldn't figure out for the life of me?

Why won't you stop crying?!

I wanted to scream it, shout it, screech it to the heavens. "She's usually so good," I croaked. My ears rang, Cora's high-pitched wails vibrating through the stuffy air.

Cam's gaze on me felt oppressive. He said nothing, but of course he was judging me. Who wouldn't? Why couldn't I get my daughter to *stop crying*?

I couldn't catch my breath. Why was it so hot? I yanked at the collar of my onesie and pushed to my feet. Cora's screams filled my head, and there was no room left to think or breathe. I couldn't leave her—didn't want to leave her—but I couldn't do this.

Anna was right.

Uncle Steve was right.

What was I thinking? I had no business taking care of a baby. I was useless! She was upset, and I couldn't fix it.

I can't do it.

I can't do it!

Cam gripped my shoulders, the pressure strangely comforting. He was saying something I couldn't make out over Cora's cries and the buzzing in my brain.

Then I was sitting on the side of the bed with Cam towering over me, his hands still on my shoulders. He spoke again, and I read his lips.

"Breathe."

With a shudder, my lungs expanded, and the buzzing faded. Cam nodded, and I inhaled again. Cora hiccupped, and I scooped her up. "It's okay," I mumbled. "I'm here."

Gently, Cam pressed the back of his big hand to her forehead. "I think she's just warm because she's worked up."

My heart still hammered my ribs, but I could breathe again as Cora's cries subsided. I sat with her on my lap on Cam's bed, and I drank the cool glass of water he pressed into my hand. Holding Cora in my arms, I inhaled her sweet, powdery scent as she finally—*finally*—settled.

"You're doing it," Cam said.

I blinked up at him. "What?"

He waved his hand. "Before, you said you can't do it. But you can."

Apparently, I'd spewed my existential parental angst aloud. *Sh—oot.* "Sorry about all…that. This." I hadn't had a nervous breakdown since the first week after bringing Cora home from the hospital. I'd thought it was one and done.

"You don't need to apologize." Cam's words hung between us, and he pressed his lips together, suddenly turning back to the fire.

The awkward tension returned in an instant. It was like we were doing some kind of strange dance. Two strangers—but not strangers—stuck in a room together with a baby, a dog, and emotional baggage piled higher than the Rockies.

After nestling Cora under the blanket in the drawer, keeping my hand over her, grounding her as her eyes closed, I whispered, "I really do need to apologize."

Cam sat abruptly in the rocker, not facing me. "It won't change anything."

"That's true." I wanted more water, but Cora still fidgeted under my spread hand. If I moved, she might wake and start crying again. "But…"

Over the years, I'd imagined what I'd say if I ever came face to face with Cam again. Well, his back was to me in the chair, but it would have to do.

I said, "That day, I—"

"*Stop.*" Cam stood to face me, backlit by the fire in the stove. Darkness had fallen completely while Cora and I had melted down.

"I told you I don't want to hear it. The only reason you want to apologize is to make yourself feel better." Cam's face was shadowed, but I could hear his clenched jaw in every word.

Wincing, I opened my mouth, but the protests died on my tongue. "You're right."

"What do you want from me?"

"Nothing. I mean—no, that's not true. I want to explain. I guess I want you to listen."

"There's no excuse for what you did."

"Agreed!" I leapt to my feet, holding my breath

as I watched Cora. She fidgeted with a grimace but was finally falling asleep. I kept my voice low.

"It was inexcusable. Unacceptable. It's the worst thing I've ever done in my life, and I wish I could change it. We both know I can't. I guess what I want is for you to know how fucking sorry I am." I glanced guiltily at Cora. "Fudging. No, fucking! I'm so *fucking* sorry, Cam."

He watched me for an uncomfortably long time before replying in a low tone, "No, Jake. You can't drop into my life out of nowhere with your pretty eyes and apologies. It's too late."

My heart sank even as my breath caught. I stupidly said, "You think my eyes are pretty?"

Cam hissed, "That's not the point! And before you tell me you're flattered, I don't need your straight guy generosity."

"I'm not straight."

He scoffed, motioning to Cora.

It was my turn for my jaw to clench. "Bisexual people can have babies. For that matter, so can gay people, but whatever. I'm bi."

"Bullshit."

I forced a deep inhale and exhale. "It's not, actually. I didn't know in high school, but I should have. I'm bi."

Cam shook his head. "You're screwing with me."

My indignation morphed into confusion.

"Why would I do that?"

"For old time's sake?"

We both clearly wanted to shout, or at least raise our voices, but we were having a whisper fight because of Cora. Whining, Toby scratched at the closed bathroom door.

"You think after you literally saved our lives that I'd want to hurt you?" The knot in my stomach tightened. "It makes me sick to think that I almost killed her." My eyes burned. "Cam, I owe you everything."

He turned away, opening and closing the stove door, the metal scraping.

"And I never, ever wanted to hurt you. I know I did, but it wasn't what I wanted. It wasn't fun. I don't blame you for thinking the worst of me, but I didn't want to hurt you then, and I don't now. And I don't get why me being bi upsets you, but—"

"It doesn't!"

"*Stop*," I hissed. "It clearly does! Why?"

"Because you know I want you!" Cam balled his hands into fists.

"I..." All I could do was blink at him. "You 'want' me? Present tense?"

Cam growled, which shouldn't have turned me on—and most definitely did. I took a step closer to the hearth, trying to smother the unexpected burst of desire. My heart thundered in my ears, and my dick was hard in an instant.

"I want you too," I whispered in the orange firelight. As I said the words, I knew they were true.

Cam closed the distance between us with a stride—and kept walking. At the door, he tugged on his boots.

Disappointment crashed through me. "Where are you going?" I watched him zip his coat and fumble with his toque and gloves. "It's dangerous out there."

Cam snorted, a sort of humorless laugh, before thudding the door shut behind him, an icy whirl of air snaking through the cabin.

After partially covering Cora's drawer with a blanket to make sure she was out of the draft, I opened the door. Night had fallen—or slammed down like a rockslide. It wasn't only dark, but another snow squall left zero visibility. I couldn't tell if it was actually still snowing or if it was simply the wind blowing it.

I pushed the door shut and brushed snow from the onesie. Cam had surely gone to check on his horse in the barn. He knew his way.

The minutes ticked by like hours.

Cora was asleep, and I automatically lay down next to her on the bed even though I wasn't tired at all. That wasn't true—I was exhausted. But my stomach gurgled with acid, and I was way too wired. There was no way I was napping. I let Toby out of the bathroom, and we both paced.

When he barked and started pawing at the front door, I hurried over and opened it, bracing against the gust of snow. Toby bolted out, disappearing immediately in the maelstrom.

"Cam?" I called.

The howling wind was the only answer.

Chapter Seven

JAKE

"CAM!"

Heart thudding, I waited. I'd shouted three times now, the sound seemingly swallowed immediately by the snow. Reaching for the two light switches on the wall, I flipped them, gratified when one illuminated an outdoor light over the door.

Inside, I turned on every light I could in case it helped Cam find his way back. Not that I even knew he was lost or missing. But each passing minute increased my nausea.

Cora was asleep, and I piled pillows and blankets to create a fort around her on the bed to block the wind from the open door.

Snow blew inside, my feet in the onesie getting wet as I stood there, arms crossed, blinking in the biting wind.

"Toby'll bring him back," I said. My voice was hoarse. I needed more water, but I remained shivering in the doorway. Toby had heard something I couldn't, and dogs had an amazing sense of hearing and smell. He'd be able to get back.

What if Cam's hurt?

I glanced back at Cora. I couldn't leave her. Even if I wouldn't get immediately disoriented and lost, I had to stay with her. There was no question.

But dread sank through me, seeping into every pore. I couldn't even call for help. Even if the phone was working—no one could come in zero visibility. Search and rescue would have to wait until the storm finally cleared.

Shivering, I squinted into the void and called again for Cam. He could have been ten feet away, and I wouldn't be able to see him. Toby would have sniffed him out, though. He had to be farther away.

What if he was stranded the way Cora and I had been? He'd come to our rescue, but all I could do was stand there uselessly in reindeer pajamas. I tugged on my gloves, keeping the door half closed and hoping the light from inside would still shine through.

Had he gone to check on the yaks? There was so much more I wanted to ask about them. So much more I wanted to ask about...everything.

He had to be okay. Maybe he wasn't even lost at all, and I was being an overemotional drama queen.

"Just *come back*," I mumbled, repeating it like a prayer. "Come back, come back, come back."

Toby's bark preceded the moment Cam's hulking figure emerged. A full-body shudder of sweet relief ran through me, and I bent to pet Toby as he appeared at my feet, tail wagging as if this was all a game. I shuffled back so Cam could squeeze inside.

He grunted as I threw my arms around him. "Are you okay?" I demanded. "God, you scared me."

Wait, I was hugging Cam. And he was letting me even though his arms still hung at his sides.

For a blissful moment, I held on.

Then Cam leaned against the closed door, his eyes shutting for a moment. His face was red, icy snow stuck to his eyelashes and crusted in his beard. I pulled off my gloves and reached up automatically to brush the snow from his face.

Cupping Cam's cheeks, the heat of my touch melted the ice crystals clinging to his beard. "Are you hurt?" I asked urgently.

His gaze met mine. He shook his head, but didn't dislodge my hands. My thumbs brushed the corners of his mouth, and I couldn't remember ever wanting to kiss someone quite this badly.

"Were you lost?" I whispered.

"I made it to the barn to check on Bonnie. Should have stayed there. I got turned around. Thanks for letting Toby out. And putting on the lights."

"Of course."

I still held his face. I'd only have to close a few inches between us, and I could kiss him. Could press our mouths together and breathe him in. Lick across his lips and slide my tongue inside. Taste him and rub my cock against him. I leaned closer. Closer…

Would he kiss me back?

Would he yank me close?

Was he hard too?

"Why did you do it?" Cam asked, barely a whisper.

The inches between us instantly transformed into a chasm. I stepped back, almost slipping on the melting snow. Cam still leaned against the door, Toby at our feet. Cam's eyes were locked on mine.

He was listening, and I finally had my chance after so many years.

"I knew as soon as I let go of that baggie that it was a horrible mistake. I was afraid I'd actually pass out. I prayed that they'd leave. That they wouldn't find anything."

Cam's smile was sharp as a razor. "Unfortunately for me, sniffer dogs are very good at their job."

"Yeah." I swallowed thickly. "I didn't know they'd have dogs. I just heard Rick Langlois say 'drug search!' and they were already coming. It was only pot, but they were cracking down."

Before I knew what I was doing, I gripped Cam's thick arms through his coat. The fabric was icy under my sweaty palms.

"God, Cam, I'm so, so sorry. You deserved so much more. From me, from the school. From everyone. Especially from me. You were such a sweet kid. I—I wasn't sure, but I think I knew you had a crush on me. You did, right?"

Cam's arms were like iron in my hands. He'd gone so still that I wasn't sure if he was breathing. He stared at me with vulnerable eyes, his shield finally down.

I pushed on. "It wasn't something I'd really *thought* about, but deep down I knew. Or at least suspected because of the way kids teased you."

Still frozen, he didn't deny it.

"You were so sweet. Geeky. Innocent. I remember thinking that your locker was the perfect hiding place. That they'd never look there. It happened so fast. One second, I thought it, and I could hear their boots on the linoleum, and my heart was going to pound right out of my chest, and I just crammed the baggie through one of the vents."

I was squeezing his arms too hard, but it felt like the only thing keeping me from shattering. Cam still didn't move a muscle. His eyes were locked on mine.

"I ran to class," I rasped. "Didn't look back. I couldn't believe it when they knocked on Mrs. Patterson's door and called your name. And you were saying it wasn't yours. Your voice went so high, and you were looking at me, completely panicked. Waiting for me to help. Did you know then it was mine?"

"Not yet," Cam muttered, his voice gravelly.

"I just sat there. Terrified. I was such a coward. If I'd spoken up then and there, it might have changed everything. But I waited a week. A *week*."

Cam's brows met, and though he still didn't move under my grip, he asked, "What do you mean?"

"It was a week later when I went to the cops. I couldn't eat. Barely slept. My parents kept asking what was wrong, and finally I told them everything. They brought me to the station, and I talked to two cops, but they said the charges had been dropped against you. That I had a promising future, and I should just shut up and count myself lucky."

For long moments, Cam was silent. Then he asked, "You confessed?"

I nodded. "I was scared shit—" I glanced automatically at Cora, who was still fast asleep. "I was terrified, but I couldn't live with myself. I wanted to call you, or go over to your house and tell you how sorry I was, but everyone told me to leave well enough alone. Even my parents." I winced. "They were good people, I swear! They were afraid that if I confessed to you, you'd get me expelled. But you already knew it was me by then, didn't you?"

Nostrils flaring, Cam nodded. "Sarah McKenzie saw you. The whispers flew all around town, but…you were you. I was me. Everyone knew you did it, but you were the baseball star. Even though you were graduating, and the season was over, how would it look if the hero of the provincial playoffs victory was a criminal? It would ruin the legacy. So you went to graduation, and I wasn't allowed."

Unlike that awful day, Cam's blue eyes were dry. Yet the hard clench of his jaw had loosened, his rigid shoulders slumping. He shrugged off my hands and removed his winter gear. I retreated to the kitchen and gulped a glass of water before pouring him one. He took it without a word.

I waited, watching Cam move stiffly to the stove and bend to open the door. The metal creaked. He shoved in another log, sparks scattering onto the stone hearth.

Cam closed the stove, locking it with the long

metal handle, the latch scraping into place. He stared, the fire burning orange beyond burnt, brown marks around the glass. I could see the side of his bearded face, the faint glow of the blaze dancing over his skin even though he stood tall. The wood popped and sizzled.

I inched closer and craned my neck to see that Cora was still sleeping, her pink lips parted, one little hand resting over her head.

When Cam finally spoke, my heart seized.

"I hated you."

I nodded. "I don't blame you."

"I knew most people didn't like me. I was the geeky gay kid. But you were different. You'd always been kind. You said hi in the hallway, and you told Travis Mosbaugh to shut up when he called me a pimply F-word. You were different."

My skin was hot with shame. "I wish I could change what I did."

"There was only a week left of school, and Principal Shore told me I was lucky I was graduating. Though I couldn't attend the ceremony. He said it would be too…controversial." Cam smiled grimly. "You want to know why I wasn't expelled or charged? Mr. Pinter intervened. My mother called him, beside herself."

I'd thought it was because it was only a tiny baggie of pot. That the authorities had realized it was ridiculous to actually arrest a kid over it. Still,

I'd known it was a risk. I'd only ever smoked up twice before, but I'd felt so grown-up with graduation approaching. What a joke. I was barely a grown-up now in my thirties.

I asked, "Where is your mother? You haven't mentioned her."

"She remarried a few years ago. Moved to Vancouver Island. Tofino. She's really into crystals and yoga. We talk once a week, and she visited last year. She's on a South American cruise right now."

"Mr. Pinter talked to the cops?"

Cam nodded. "He has power. Money talks and all that. He's a good man, though. The best. He offered me a summer job on the ranch. He'd offered before, but I always thought it was out of obligation. I was so scrawny—not exactly ranch hand material. After what he did for me, I was the one who felt obligated. I never expected to fall in love with it. Since my university admission was revoked, I stayed on. I grew and started working out." He shrugged as if to say, *the rest is history*.

"Reinvented yourself."

"I guess."

"And…came out?"

Cam took a deep breath and exhaled slowly with a nod. "My mom and Mr. and Mrs. Pinter accepted me." He stooped to nuzzle Toby. "Toby, Bonnie, and the yaks don't care."

"I'm so thankful to the Pinters. Cam, I… I

know I can never make it up to you, but I'd love to try. If there's anything—*anything*—I can do, please tell me."

Cam straightened and stared at me. "I believe you. That you're sorry. Kids make mistakes. We're not kids anymore."

As if to punctuate that statement, Cora stirred with a grumble and grunt. Cam laughed softly, and my heart swelled with hope. I wasn't even sure what I was hopeful for, but as I warmed Cora's formula and Cam made sloppy joes, the future didn't seem quite so scary.

Chapter Eight

CAM

EARLY ON CHRISTMAS Eve, I woke to the hum of the white noise app on Jake's phone. Though I was used to utter silence aside from Toby's snuffling breaths, I'd dropped right off and slept well aside from waking briefly when Jake had gotten up with Cora.

In the days since Jake and Cora had arrived, Toby and I had apparently gotten used to their presence.

Had that only been *two days* ago?

The whole world had narrowed down to the four walls of my cabin. It felt like we'd been here together for years.

As I thought of Jake, I tensed automatically, my mind replaying all the things we'd said. The tension ebbed away with a fresh wave of relief. I'd clung to my resentment for so long that it felt like an amputation to let it go. But a welcome one.

What was that saying about resentment being like drinking poison and waiting for the other person to die?

Even when Jake's parents had been killed, I hadn't allowed my anger to ease. Even though I'd rarely thought of him as the years went on, the resentment had remained like a pilot light, ready to flare to life with a spark.

Quietly, I stashed the bedroll and stoked the fire in the stove. Toby looked up from his spot on the hearth, then returned to snoozing. As orange light brightened the room a few degrees, I watched Jake in my bed, his back to me, curled toward his daughter in the drawer.

I waited.

The resentment that had smoldered for half my life had finally burned itself out after its final blaze.

When good, loyal Toby had raced into the whiteout and led me back to the cabin, I'd spotted first the flicker of light, then finally Jake silhouetted in the doorway in the silly reindeer pajamas. My relief at returning to the safety of my cabin had been followed by a surge of emotion I still couldn't name.

I'd been alone with my animals for so long. I'd told myself I didn't need anyone else. Didn't want anyone else. Certainly not *Jake Gregson*. But returning to him—the warmth of his worried embrace, the gentle touch of his hands on my face—had left me shaken.

The fire warmed my back as I stood watching him sleep. His lips were parted, one hand reaching toward Cora. In my replaying of everything we'd said, four words lingered.

"*I want you too.*"

I escaped to the bathroom to piss and get my shit together before I went full creep mode with watching him sleep and wondering what his lips would taste like, and if his nipples were sensitive, and did he like giving head? And, and and…

I showered, very glad of the powerful water heater I'd indulged in—and Mr. Pinter's great deal on that generator. I resisted jerking off, but only because I heard Cora's sleepy morning cries and it didn't feel right.

I hadn't brought any clothes into the bathroom, so I opened the door in my terrycloth robe.

Cradling a fussy Cora while her bottle heated, Jake looked over from the kitchen. His Adam's apple bobbed before he rasped, "Morning." He watched me, waiting.

"Morning. Hope I didn't wake you." It was still before six.

Jake exhaled, smiling. "Nope. It was this one." He nuzzled her head. "Someone's hungry, as usual." He shifted her to one arm to check the milk, reaching for the bottle awkwardly.

"Here." I rushed over to help.

"Thanks." Jake's even teeth gleamed under the kitchen light as I tested the formula on my wrist.

When I looked up to hand over the bottle, Jake's gaze snapped up to my face. He took the bottle quickly and cooed to Cora, encouraging her to drink. I glanced down to see that my robe had gaped open, barely closed at my waist. It was a little too small, but it'd been the biggest the store in Lonely Creek stocked.

"*I want you too.*"

Voice low, Jake asked, "Um, what's it look like out there? Do you think…"

My simmering excitement turned to a nervous swoop in my gut. I hadn't even thought about it, and now that I did, I hadn't noticed the wind howling. Snow was piled up against the window, and in the dark, it was hard to see anything.

I crossed to the door, bracing as I opened it. The icy wind still blasted.

The relief was sweet and swift. Sure, it had died down, but not enough. I cleared my throat. "Still iffy. I think it stopped snowing, but visibility could drop to zero anytime. It's not safe to get to my truck, let alone on the road."

The wind had slowed compared to yesterday, but whiteouts really could happen in a blink. I shuddered to think of being stuck out there waiting for Toby to find me. I'd made the trip to the barn and back a million times, but my head had been spinning, and I truly hadn't been able to see a damn thing.

The idea of Jake and Cora being outside in a whiteout made me sick to my stomach. They'd have to stay at least another day.

With Cora safe in his arms suckling her bottle, Jake nodded. "Better safe than sorry, right?" He took a step and grimaced.

"What?" I asked as I closed the door behind me, eager to shut out the rest of the world. I should have let Jake apologize right away. We'd wasted a day when we could have been—

Stop right there.

My fantasies were running wild, like a dam had been released. I refocused on Jake, who was shaking his onesie-covered foot.

"Feet are still a bit damp."

I must've looked as puzzled as I felt, because Jake added, "There was snow blowing in the doorway while you were outside and I was waiting."

"Why didn't you say?" I opened my bottom drawer and fished out gray sweats and a T-shirt. I grabbed a fresh pair of socks as well.

"I don't want to go through all your PJs. Do you have laundry?" His forehead creased as he glanced around.

"The Pinters' housekeeper does mine every couple of weeks. I'll have my own in the new house, though."

"Oh, right! You're moving." He shifted Cora upright and patted her back. "This place is great, though." He kicked his foot again.

"I'll take her. Get changed." I held out my hands.

His full lips quirked into a smile. "Yeah, okay."

Cora babbled as I lifted her into my arms, reaching out a tiny hand to my beard. She'd dribbled formula onto her green elephant onesie, and I swiped at it with my finger. Jake watched us, laughing when Cora reached for my chest hair through the V of my robe.

"You've got a bit more than me," he said, then seemed to shake himself. He picked up the folded sweats from the bed—then unzipped the reindeer onesie.

I spun to face the kitchen, concentrating on tracing the delicate shell of Cora's ear.

"What's the new house going to look like?" Jake asked from behind me. "I can't picture you in one of those McMansions."

"Definitely not. Two stories. Three bedrooms. Wraparound porch. Uh, a kitchen and a couple of bathrooms."

He chuckled. "I'd hope there'd be a kitchen. What style did you go with?"

I patted Cora's back, but she only gurgled and babbled. No burp yet. "It's…nice. There's one of those islands."

Jake chuckled. "Ah, the 'nice' style. I have a feeling the porch is your favorite part. Oh, and is there a fireplace? You need a spot for your rocker."

I had to laugh. "Guilty as charged."

Fabric *shushed* behind me. "I wonder what my house looks like now." Immediately, he added, "Not *my* house. I mean my uncle's."

There was a hitch in his tone that made me turn. I was momentarily speechless at the sight of his bare chest. "Uh, the rental where you're staying, you mean?" I frowned, trying to figure out what had put that tension in Jake's voice. I watched him reach up and pull my too-big T-shirt over his head, his lean pecs and dark nipples bared before the cotton dropped. "Where is it, again?"

"Hamilton Street."

"That's where you used to live."

Jake rubbed his face, stubble scratching under his palm. He didn't have a full beard, but it would still rub against mine. Create friction, and…

Cora burped and farted. Smiling, Jake reached for her. "Very classy, darling."

Retying the belt of my robe, I asked, "Is this rental close to where you grew up?"

Jake bounced Cora and sighed. "Yeah, it's my house." He winced. "No, it's my uncle's house.

But it's where I grew up."

"Your parents didn't leave it to you?"

He smiled tightly. "No, they did. But at the time, I was in school in Toronto. I had no plans to ever move home. It was hardly worth anything back then. I sold it to my uncle and used the money to pay my tuition and expenses. He renovated and turned it into multiple apartments when vacation rentals really took off. It was smart. It looks nice on Airbnb."

I took this in. "You're going to live in the basement of the house you grew up in?"

"Yeah, it'll be a little weird." Jake's smile was forced. "I'm just lucky he agreed to take the basement off the rental sites. I definitely need to figure out where I'm going before ski season starts again next year. The real estate market has exploded everywhere. But I didn't know that would happen back then."

"Right. No way you could have known."

Jake swallowed hard. "My parents were gone, and the last thing I wanted was our empty house."

I nodded.

Before Jake could say anything else, Cora grunted and squirmed, and a new smell filled the air. Jake put on a cheerful tone. "It's diaper time!"

Toby and I headed to the barn as the sun rose, and I brushed down Bonnie and gave her treats. As she crunched her apple core, Toby burrowed into snow drifts having the time of his life.

The morning sky was still gray, and thick cloud cover threatened more snowfall. Even if it was done for now, it would take ages for them to dig out of the storm and plow the roads.

The power was likely still out in Lonely Creek, and tomorrow was Christmas. Best to wait at least until Boxing Day to venture out. It was the only logical thing to do.

I gritted my teeth as I mucked out Bonnie's stall and thought of Jake's *former* house in town. While it was true that it belonged to this uncle of his now, and that the man had every right to do with it as he pleased and charge rent...

It didn't sit right. Not at all. I couldn't imagine how strange it would be to go live in the basement of my childhood home. Mom had sold it when she remarried, and I didn't even know who lived there now.

But the idea of returning to that place where my dad had barbecued in the yard all year round with a light beer in his hand while my mom sang along to Garth Brooks and baked the best chocolate chip cookies in the world...

Where Dad and I had strung blinking Christmas lights across the eaves and porch and all the way up the massive fir in our front yard. Was the tree still there? For all I knew, that house had been torn down to make way for something bigger.

Even in Lonely Creek, I'd spotted new McMansions, as Jake had called them.

Outside the open barn door, Toby barked, chasing his own tail like a cartoon, snow flying everywhere. I laughed and called him over to give him a treat from my pocket before I filled Bonnie's hay net in her stall.

"*I want you too.*"

Christ, I had to get a hold of myself. Jake's words haunted me. I hadn't bothered getting laid for going on two years, but here I was fighting erections like I was back in high school.

Had the heat I'd spotted in his eyes when he'd removed the sliver been real? Though I'd been a horse's ass about it, 'course I knew bisexuality was legit.

I'd never been fussed about labels, but Jake's return had me thinking. Aside from a few half-hearted hookups over the years, it was just me, Toby, Bonnie, and the yaks. None of them gave a shit about labels, but... Was there a word for me?

I tried to remember the last time I'd been this hot for a guy. It wasn't like I hadn't gotten my rocks off from time to time, but I could usually take it or leave it. Had it ever been this roaring fire in my blood?

I wanted to kiss Jake until we couldn't breathe. Suck his nipples and his cock and eat his ass and fuck him and make him come until he couldn't stand and—

Head tilted, Toby barked at me. Christ, I was hard as a rock, and if it wasn't freezing, I'd have yanked out my dick right there to relieve the pressure. Though maybe not with Toby and Bonnie watching.

Quickly, I dug through my storage shed for a box Mrs. Pinter had given me years ago before trudging back through the snow to the cabin.

Jake was down on the carpet with Cora, singing about a purple monkey while she pushed up on her hands and tried to roll over again. I stamped my boots as Toby raced over to lick Cora and Jake like he hadn't seen them in years.

Jake wrapped his arms around a snowy Toby to keep him from Cora, laughing and squirming. I called off Toby but couldn't stop smiling.

As I fried up eggs and bacon, the salty, greasy sizzle filled the cabin. It was ridiculous that I didn't have a proper table. Hell, I didn't even own two chairs. Mrs. Pinter had reminded me before they left that furniture could take months to arrive and I was overdue on picking it out. She'd left me fliers and catalogs that were still on my dresser under my newest books.

Jake insisted he was fine on the rug, and I let Toby back out so he wouldn't hound Jake for his bacon. I sat in my rocker and listened as Jake told me about why purple monkeys in trees were a thing. Then he explained six-month milestones in baby development while Cora chewed on a stuffed tiger.

"I'm sorry." His face flushed. "This is so boring."

"It's not," I said. "It's the same with yaks. They have milestones as they grow. Uh…not that Cora's the same as a yak."

"Less hairy," Jake replied seriously. "So far, at least."

The morning passed, and I couldn't remember the last time I'd had a day off like this. Sure, I hadn't worked the day before, but Jake had been walking on eggshells, and we hadn't talked much. I'd had a neck ache from being tense.

Today, I could breathe.

It took a while for Cora to stop fussing and drift off, and Jake carried her drawer to the bathroom, placing it carefully on the floor with his phone playing the white noise. "I want to make sure she gets enough sleep," he whispered. He tucked her in and pulled the door half closed.

Then he exhaled, his shoulders dropping. He closed his eyes for a moment, leaning against the door jamb. The months of sleep deprivation showed. I could see the way he poured all his energy into Cora and left barely anything for himself.

I straightened from where I stoked the fire and

returned the poker to its stand. When I flipped off the kitchen light, only weak, cloudy daylight came through the one window and combined with the fire's flickering orange glow.

Jake watched me. "Um, is Toby still okay out there?" he asked, still whispering.

I nodded.

"Cool."

"You should nap."

He sighed. "Yeah, that's what they say. Sleep when she sleeps. I just…" He scratched his neck, his fingers moving over his collarbone in the loose opening of my shirt. "It's like, all I do is baby stuff." He straightened suddenly. "And I love it!" He glanced behind into the bathroom and lowered his voice. "I love her."

"I know." I realized belatedly that his feet were bare again. "Where are your socks?"

He looked down. "Oh, I spilled formula on one." He motioned to the socks hanging off the headboard. I hadn't even noticed—probably because I hadn't been able to take my eyes off Jake.

I brushed past him—did Jake's breath hitch?—and grabbed another pair from the overstuffed drawer. "Here."

Our fingers met over the ball of wool.

Eyes dark and locked on mine, Jake murmured, "Thanks."

We stood staring in the dim light. Blood

rushed in my ears, and I waited. Jake was supposed to put on the socks now.

Instead, his gaze flicked between my eyes and my lips, and—

Our mouths crushed together.

I was drowning. Drowning in *him*. Years ago, I'd imagined kissing Jake Gregson a million times. Imagined *him* kissing *me*. He'd been so confident and tall and awe-inspiring.

Now, he clung to me, his fingers digging into my biceps, gasping as I thrust my tongue into his mouth. I pulled him close, one hand behind his head, my fingers tangling in his thick, wavy hair. He tasted like bacon and black coffee, and we kissed until I had to suck in a breath.

Lips shiny, Jake blinked up at me. "Who would've thought little Cam Walsh could kiss like that?"

I couldn't help it—I puffed up. "Not so little now."

"Oh, I noticed." He ran his hands down my arms, then up under my sweater, his fingers spreading over my ribs. I shivered at the light touch. Jake bit his lip the way he had when taking out the sliver. "Can I see you?"

Pulse thrumming, I yanked off my sweater and jeans too quickly. Too eagerly? But Jake didn't seem to mind, his gaze locked on the bulge of my hard cock in my white boxer briefs. Slowly, he traced his fingertips along my shaft through the cotton.

Pleasure and pride and desire sparking through me, I lifted the hem of the T-shirt he wore, and Jake lifted his arms. With a step back, he was sitting on the end of the bed in only my sweats, the socks forgotten. Looking up at me, he swallowed hard.

"Are you—have you been tested?" he asked. "I haven't been with anyone since Anna. I got tested a few times after I found out she'd cheated, and she did too. I'm good."

I nodded. "Clear over a year ago. No one since."

A smile ghosted his full lips. "Just you and the animals out here, huh?"

"The yaks aren't my type."

He laughed, then bit into his lip, breathing hard.

"What do you want?" I asked, practically growling. It was all I could do not to leap on him.

"Um…" Something flickered over his expression, his brow creasing. His eyes flicked to the bathroom door, which was still half closed. Cora wasn't visible. The only sound was the distant hum of the white noise app.

"It's okay," I murmured, running my hand over his soft hair.

Eyes closing, he leaned into the touch and

reached out, his fingers finding my thighs at the bottom of my underwear.

"What do you want?" I repeated, straining like a racehorse at the gate.

Jake flickered with tension again. He dropped his face as he stuttered, "I—I, um…"

Unease slithered through me like icy water. I lifted Jake's chin—and staggered back at the tears shining in his brown eyes.

"I'm sorry!" He rubbed his face. "Fuck. Fudge. *Fuck.*"

"What is this?" I asked hoarsely. "Are you…" A terrible thought seized me. "Do you not want this? Is this some…payback? Like you owe me?"

His wet eyes widened. "No! *No.*" He reached for me, but I stayed just out of grasp. "I don't know what's happening."

My stomach twisted. "I don't want your pity. Or to be your…repentance."

Jake shook his head, his hands knotting in his lap. He watched me with those big, beautiful eyes. "I want you. I just don't know…" He shook his head again. "I don't know why I'm crying." He swiped at his cheeks. "You asked a simple question, and I'm having a meltdown." His gaze slipped to the bathroom door.

Tentatively, I stepped close again and caressed his head. Jake leaned into me, throwing his arms around my waist. I slipped my arm around the warm skin of his back as he pressed his damp cheek to my stomach.

I slowly stroked his head, murmuring, "It's okay."

"Really sexy, huh?" he mumbled.

"It's okay," I repeated.

Jake leaned back and peered up at me seriously. "Can you just…" His brows met. "You asked what I wanted, and it's like… I make so many decisions every day. For her. It's all on me. Am I using the right formula? The right diapers? Is she warm enough? Is she too warm? Is she hungry? Did I feed her too much? Is she sick? Should I have kept her inside? Or taken her out to get fresh air? It never stops."

Jake closed his eyes, then opened them. "I just want someone to tell me what to do. I don't know what I want. Except you. I know I want you. Please."

"You want me to tell you what to do?"

He nodded eagerly and licked his lips.

Forget presents under the tree—helping him felt like the greatest gift. My mind spun with the possibilities. With Jake at the end of the bed staring up at me waiting, his gaze raking over my body, I found myself saying two simple words.

"Watch me."

Jake's lips parted as his breath hitched. He nodded, licking his lips. I stepped back so we weren't touching, the air between us electric.

My cock swelled again under Jake's excited gaze. I teased myself through the cotton, the fabric straining until I had to tug it down and kick off the briefs. Naked, I stood in front of Jake. No longer the scrawny kid. I wanted him to *see* me.

The flushed head of my cock poked out of my foreskin. I stroked my shaft, forcing myself to go slowly. Jake opened and closed his mouth, maybe trying to speak or simply breathe. A flush rose from his chest. Brown hair scattered his pecs, his nipples dark and hard.

The flush traveled all the way up his face, though it was clear his body had diverted a significant amount of blood southward. His— *my*—track pants tented with the bulge of his erection, and my blood sang with lust.

Inside, teenage me crowed with pride that *I* was making Jake hard. Just at the sight of me! Only my arm moved as I fisted my cock. I'd never had a voyeurism kink before, but *damn*, the way his eyes were glued to me. Spreading my legs, I arched my spine.

I was putting on a show. There was no other way to describe it. Jake watched me toy with the head of my cock, electric pulses rippling through my groin. He watched me circle my nipples until they were sharp and rake my blunt nails through my chest hair. He watched me fondle my balls as I stroked my shaft harder with my other hand.

And I watched Jake.

The wet spot darkened the light gray of his tented sweats. His hands were fisted at his sides. His chest heaved, his skin still red. He didn't touch himself. He gasped through shiny, parted lips. His eyes still glistened, though the tears were unshed. Even though I was the naked one, it was Jake who was defenseless. Breakable.

I didn't want him to break.

Power surged through me. *Control.* I was letting Jake watch me, and it was my show. *Me.* Dorky, loser, laughable *me.* Even though that hadn't been me in years, my teenaged self had never fully gone away. And it made me so hot that Jake wanted me.

A jagged moan tore out of my throat, my chest burning. My balls tightened, toes curling on the cold floor. I grunted and groaned and watched Jake's beautiful face as I came.

Drops splattered his chest, marking him. White-hot pleasure roared through my veins, and I milked my cock with both hands, eyes locked on Jake. He still hadn't touched himself, but he shuddered as I worked my prick, tremors rocking his rigid body.

I sank down at Jake's feet, the wood floor solid under my knees. My hands hovered in the air by his hips as he stared at me, still frozen.

I told him, "I'm going to drink your cum," and waited.

The sound Jake made was part moan, part gasp, part whine. He nodded hard.

I'd imagined this back in the day. Not just having Jake's cock in my mouth—which I did after yanking down the sweats to his thighs. I sucked him with a groan, digging my fingers into his hips. He was uncut too, and I teased at his foreskin.

Hell yeah, I'd imagined this—Jake's long dick almost in my throat, my lips stretched around his meat as he moaned. I'd imagined his pubes tickling my nose, my tongue winding around him. Pulling back to play with the head.

What I hadn't known was how he'd shake and whimper. How I'd want to protect him and help him get off because he clearly needed it so much. How could I have realized I'd want to soothe him and tell him everything would be all right?

Not that I could tell Jake anything with my mouth crammed full of him, spit dribbling from my stretched lips.

But what I'd imagined too many times to count was Jake coming in my mouth. Over the years, I hadn't let many guys do that. It had happened from time to time, but usually I pulled off. But I'd never felt like this with any other guy. I'd never been so consumed with lust.

I wanted to swallow him whole.

But I also wasn't quite ready for it to be over yet. Panting, I pulled off and sat back on my heels between Jake's spread legs as he whimpered. I ran my fingers over his shaking thighs, hair tickling my skin. One after the other, I lapped at his balls, rubbing my beard against the soft skin of his inner thighs.

He tangled one hand in my hair, and shivers ran down my spine. Lifting my head, I whispered, "I want you to come for me."

I sucked hard on his cock, and he did as he was told, arching and coming with a muffled shout. My mouth flooded with musky, bitter cum, and I swallowed thirstily.

Jake had finally broken, but I was holding him together.

I looked up to find him watching me, his chest rising and falling heavily. I was still holding his thighs as he brushed his fingertips over my swollen lips.

I didn't have to tell him to lean down and kiss me.

Chapter Nine

JAKE

WHEN WAS THE last time I'd woken in bed with someone else?

Someone who wasn't my baby girl?

After Anna left me, I'd had a few hookups, the last with a man and woman looking for a bi guy. It had been fun, but there'd been no snuggling. That had been before Cora was born, which felt like a different life.

Now? There was snuggling.

Eyes still closed, I was curled into Cam's side with his arm around me, my cheek against his hairy chest. Was he asleep? I couldn't tell. There'd been no time to worry about things getting awkward after our orgasms faded because Cam had immediately drawn me into bed and pulled the covers over us.

Maybe waking in his arms should have been

uncomfortable—it was certainly a tight squeeze on the double mattress—but after what we'd just shared, we were loose and languid.

Though excitement fizzed through me now as I replayed it. *God, watching Cam like that*—so powerful yet somehow vulnerable.

Raw.

He'd been beautiful. And the sight of him dropping to his knees and sucking my cock like a starving man would live rent-free in my head until the end of time.

I stirred, rubbing my stubble against his nipple. His low chuckle under my ear was beyond sexy.

You know what wasn't? *Crying.* I cringed as I remembered that part.

Cam caressed my spine. "What?" His voice was low. "She's still sleeping. You weren't out long. Maybe twenty minutes."

Guilt twisted through me as I realized Cora hadn't been my first thought. Well, I'd thought about her—but I hadn't checked on her. I was still warm and sleepy in Cam's arms with my eyes closed and drops of his cum dried in my chest hair.

And it was exactly where I wanted to be.

Still, I murmured, "We should…"

"Mm. Not yet."

Opening my eyes, I shifted enough to look up at him. In the afterglow, his grim, stony expression had softened into the sweetest smile. My belly flip-flopped with a warm rush of excitement and affection. Cam had always worn his heart on his sleeve.

Immediately, a voice in my head warned me not to get my hopes up. I wasn't even sure about what. God, couldn't I just enjoy a few minutes feeling warm and safe and comforted? I wanted to just share this moment with Cam. We'd have to go back to the real world soon enough.

"When did you know you were bi?" Cam asked.

I lowered my head to his chest, and he ran his big hand up and down my back as I reminisced.

"Second year of university. I saw two men at the gym one night. It was late, and I finished my reps just under the wire. Hustled into the locker room and figured I didn't have time for a shower since the staff at the front desk wanted to go home. But I stank, so I decided they'd have to wait a few more minutes."

I chuckled. "It took me an embarrassingly long time to understand what the noises were. For a second, I was afraid someone was having a heart attack or something. I went to investigate to make sure someone didn't need help."

"Mm." Cam leaned down and kissed the top of my head. He traced the curve of my ear with his fingertips.

"They were in the last stall, and the curtain was only half drawn. They were fucking. Two of the big guys I always saw around, lifting heavy and grunting. Spotting each other. They were definitely doing more grunting. One of them was braced on the tile wall with his arms and legs spread, being fucked."

"What did you do?"

"Watched. My brain was shouting at me to back away, but I couldn't take my eyes off them. I'd seen guys kissing or whatever on TV. Never thought too much about it. I was fine with it. But this was so...*real*. They were groaning, their muscles flexing with so much power. I'd admired their bodies before out on the floor. They were ripped." I looked up. "Like you."

Cam's breath punched out in a rush, his voice hoarse. "Did it make you hard?"

I nodded, still watching Cam under my lashes. "I stood there, rock hard, spying on them. They could have seen me if they'd looked back, but they were totally focused on each other. The one behind, he was kissing the other guy's neck and reaching around to jerk his dick while he pounded him. It was like I'd walked into a porno."

"It does sound a lot like one."

I laughed. "It does." I ran my hand over Cam's chest, my thumb catching on his nipple. I explored Cam's chest and belly, making him squirm and laugh when my fingers skimmed his ribs. "Ticklish, huh?"

"No," he said, even as I proved him wrong, his belly quivering under my feather-light touch. "Okay, okay. Yes."

I relented, resting my hand on his stomach, light fur under my palm.

"Did you jerk off?" he asked.

For a second, I was puzzled and going to reply that no, I hadn't, because he'd just sucked me off, before remembering what we'd been talking about. My brain was mush, but in the best way instead of my usual sleep-deprived haze.

"Oh, yeah. I stumbled away as soon as they came. Forgot the shower and shoved my hard dick in my jeans. It was a good thing it was winter and I had a long coat. Practically ran back to res. My roommate was on his way out, and I didn't even make it to my bed. Just leaned back against the door, spit on my hand, and made myself come. Started looking at guys in a whole new light after that."

"Mm. I bet." Cam drew my head up and kissed me slow and deep.

Even after sucking me, I could still taste a hint of the mint Chapstick I'd seen him slip into his pocket...yesterday? What even was time? Kissing him felt so *right*. How was that possible? I'd never put stock in the idea of fate, but kissing Cam

Walsh all these years later might have made me a believer.

Over the faint hum of white noise in the bathroom, Cora coughed and grunted. Cam and I froze, waiting. The seconds ticked by, but she settled again, and so did we.

There were things I should have been doing, like getting formula ready to go so she wouldn't have time to get cranky when she woke. But it was so warm and comfy smushed under the covers with Cam.

He held me close, and I circled his belly button with my fingertip. Cam asked quietly, "When did you decide to keep Cora? You said an adoption had been arranged."

I actually shuddered to think of it, and Cam rubbed my back gently. I figured I'd start at the beginning. "Anna's water broke at thirty-six weeks."

"What's the normal number of weeks? I know it's nine months, but… Don't make me do math."

I had to smile. "Thirty-nine or forty weeks is considered full term."

"How big was Cora when she was born?"

"Five pounds, twelve ounces."

"Whoa."

"Yeah. She was tiny. Smaller than I could have imagined. Not that I'd really pictured it. I hadn't thought about whether I'd be there for the delivery. It was a weird time. I was trying not to think about any of it. Totally in denial. I figured if Anna wanted adoption, that was that. It wasn't like I was going to be a single father and raise a baby all by myself. It seemed absurd."

Cam squeezed my bare hip, and I swallowed thickly. Thinking back to that time before Cora was born, I barely recognized myself.

"Anna's boss boyfriend didn't want to go into the room. He waited down the hall even though she was screaming in pain. I guess he was in his own denial. Her family back in Poland didn't even know she was pregnant. Anna hurt me, but I couldn't leave her alone. I held her hand and told her to push and all that stuff. Her friends came, but the hospital only allowed one person in the room. She was squeezing my hand so tightly. I couldn't let go."

As I breathed in and out, Cam nuzzled my head.

"Cora was barely breathing when she was born. They took her to the NICU right away, and one of the nurses grabbed me and told me to follow. I was there all night. She was so small compared to the machines. There were wires all over her. It's still amazing to be able to hold her without any machines attached. I knew before I left to shower and sleep for a few hours that I was keeping her."

"I can imagine."

"When I got back to the NICU, one of the nurses said, 'Hi, daddy!' They'd call the parents mom or mommy and dad or daddy—they had too many patients in and out to know our names. Every time they called me 'dad,' it stoked this new fire inside me. I've never had purpose like this. Love like this."

Caressing my back and hip with slow sweeps, Cam murmured, "Mm."

"I went to Anna's room. She was being discharged. I told her I was keeping the baby with or without her. She didn't argue."

"You're not worried she might change her mind?"

I shrugged. "Boss man got his lawyer to draw up the papers. She gave up her parental rights. If she changes her mind, I'll deal with it. But I don't think she will. She never wanted kids. I respect that. It's not easy." I had to laugh. "Understatement of the century."

"How long did you say Cora in the NICU?"

"Nine days. She had trouble eating. She couldn't suck, swallow, and breathe at the same time. She'd start turning blue, and it was..." I shuddered again.

"Jesus. I can only imagine." Cam held me tighter.

"Yeah. Since she wasn't delivered at term, she had an immature digestive and respiratory system.

She'd suck on the tiny bottle and start choking. She'd only get a bit of donated breast milk and formula down. It took practice for her to be able to eat normally. I'd be there every morning, go home and have lunch, then go back. I read books to her for hours. Hoped my voice would block out the constant beeping. There was so much noise. Some beeps were fine and regular, but some were scary. The nurses would rush over to that baby, and my heart would pound, hoping they were okay. Relieved it wasn't Cora's machines."

"It's okay. She's safe. You've taken such good care of her."

I realized I was trembling, and I blinked away tears. I turned my face into Cam's warm, solid chest and mumbled, "Thank you," against his skin.

Cora was going to wake, and it was time to get up…in just a few more minutes.

LATER THAT NIGHT after bath time, I dressed Cora in her last clean onesie. Cam and I had eaten a dinner of frozen meals together standing in the kitchen talking about yaks versus cattle. I loved listening to him, his low baritone rising when he was excited.

Fuuu*dge*, he was gorgeous.

When it was time for bed, the cabin lit only by

the fire's glow, Cam unfurled the bedroll at the foot of the bed again. Toby had settled on the hearth, and Cora was snug in the drawer on the mattress. I stood there, wearing Cam's baggy sweats again

"I want to sleep with you," I blurted. *Real smooth.*

Cam's blue eyes darkened. "Right now?"

"Yes. I mean, yes, of course I do. What I mean at the moment is just sleeping. But I don't think there's enough room."

He smiled. "It's okay. I'm good on the floor."

I bit my lip. "It's just that I've never spent a night without her next to me since she came home from the hospital."

"I understand." In his PJ bottoms and T-shirt, Cam stretched out on the floor and tugged up his blankets. "Sleep well."

I tried. I really did!

It felt like an eternity but was probably only fifteen minutes later when I slipped out of bed and crawled over Cam. His eyes popped open, and he stifled a laugh as we kissed. He tugged the blankets over me, and I straddled his hips, both of us hard already.

As I burrowed my hands under his T-shirt and spread my fingers through his chest hair, Cam whispered, "What do you want?"

Leaning low, I put my lips to his ear. "Will you

tell me what to do?"

Cam inhaled sharply and kissed me, his fingers tightening in my hair. I moaned into his kiss, rocking my hips. His mouth was hot and wet, his tongue stroking mine—

And then another tongue licked my ear.

Squirming, I slapped a hand over my mouth to muffle a laugh as Toby squeezed between us, licking our faces enthusiastically. Cam's chest rumbled with laughter, and he tried to order Toby back to the hearth.

It was no use. We couldn't stop laughing, which only encouraged Toby. I wheezed. "As much as I want you, I'm not up for a threesome."

Cam sighed and pushed away Toby's snout. "I could shut him in the bathroom, but he's not used to it."

"No, no. I don't want him to be alone." Petting Toby with one hand, I kissed Cam and nuzzled against his beard. "We can wait."

"Mm-hmm. Waited a long time already. I can wait more."

I had to kiss him, sliding my tongue into his mouth, breathing him in. Until Toby tried to join in again, and I retreated to Cam's bed. Cora was fast asleep, one arm up over her head, and I ghosted a kiss over her head before drifting away with a smile on my lips.

Chapter Ten

JAKE

THE STORM WAS definitely over, because apparently the sun was back. With my eyes still closed, I could sense golden light. When I reached blindly for Cora, she was still beside me in the drawer, her chest rising and falling. She usually woke before sunrise, but the time change had probably messed her up.

Blinking sleepily, I didn't understand what I was looking at. Then I shook off the cobwebs and sat up, gazing around the cabin in wonder. Turned out that it was indeed still early and dark outside.

But inside, sparkly ornaments hung from doorknobs, and a small artificial tree decked in little ornaments and rainbow fairy lights sat on the edge of the hearth with a glittery star on top.

"Merry Christmas," Cam said from the top of a step ladder by the foot of the bed. Still in his PJs, he was using duct tape to string golden lights on the ceiling around the cabin perimeter and was almost finished. Tail wagging, Toby circled the step ladder.

"Holy shit!" I exclaimed. "Er, shoot. Darn. Something. Whatever! This is…wow. Where did you get these?"

"Mrs. Pinter gave me a box of decorations years ago. I figured there was no sense in bothering when it was just me and Toby." He ripped off another strip of tape with his teeth, which made me incredibly horny. "Thought Cora might like it. It's her first Christmas, after all." He shrugged. "Thought you might like it too."

Careful not to jostle Cora, I crawled to the end of the bed and pushed up on my knees, reaching for Cam's flannel-covered hips. I just needed to touch him. "Thank you."

"Sure." He smoothed one hand over my messy hair. "Better the stuff gets used."

"I wish I'd kept the decorations from when I was a kid. I barely took anything when we cleaned out the house since I didn't have room in Toronto. There are a couple of boxes of pictures and stuff in Uncle Steve's garage. Assuming he hasn't tossed them, but I don't think he would. Even Uncle Steve isn't that cold."

"Jesus, I hope not." Cam stepped down to the floor and kissed me. I melted into his arms—and

Cora woke with a fussy cry.

We sighed, and I said, "Welcome to parenthood," then sputtered. "I—I didn't mean—not that you're—I was just—I should get her."

Cam nodded with an awkward chuckle "I'll finish the lights."

I'd never even thought about dating as a single father—who had the time?—but I'd scare him off in no time with talk like that.

Not that we're dating. Stop jumping ahead and just enjoy Christmas.

"The decorations really are beautiful," I said. "Thank you."

"It's nothing. They were collecting dust." Back on the step ladder, he shrugged. "I don't really know what else goes into a baby's first Christmas, but I figured decorations helped."

"I guess it's just like a normal Christmas? Unless I missed a memo on special activities." Grimacing, I lifted a squirming Cora from her drawer. "Probably did. The mommy influencers will be up at dawn baking organic gingerbread and whipping up a handcrafted stocking with locally sourced felt."

Cam made a show of checking his watch. "It's not too late."

In my arms, Cora settled for the moment, so I relaxed back against the headboard and snuggled under the covers. "We would always have pancakes

Christmas morning. Blueberry. Then my parents would bicker about the syrup because my dad loved the fake kind."

Cam wrinkled his nose, which was all kinds of adorable. "No, no. It has to be maple syrup. That fake sugar liquid is...unCanadian."

"Agreed! But Dad loved it. And Mom would complain, but there was always a bottle in the pantry at Christmas."

Cam hung the last length of lights with a final sexy rip of tape. "The mommy people on the internet definitely use duct tape, right?"

"Absolutely. It's industrial chic Christmas."

Cam's teeth flashed as he smiled under the golden lights, and my *god*, he was absolutely gorgeous.

I asked, "What did you have for breakfast Christmas morning? Growing up, I mean."

"Hm." He sat on the side of the bed, idly rubbing my knee through the duvet. "Usually just cereal. Dad had to be out here with the herd some Christmases, so we'd wait until he got home to open presents. We didn't have much lunch because turkey and stuffing were coming." His thumb circled my kneecap. "Pancakes sound awfully good, though."

I brightened. "We could make some."

"We could?" He raised a dubious brow.

As Cora grunted, I said, "Sure. It can't be that

hard."

"What's in pancakes?"

"Um…flour?"

"Yep, sounds right."

"Some kind of milk? Maybe some of that baking powder. Or the other one. Soda? Maybe baking soda. And blueberries, or whatever you want to put in."

"Right. So, I don't have any of those things."

We laughed, and Cora wriggled and squawked. I had to get up and start her routine, but it was so warm under the covers, and Cam's hand was heavy and comforting.

He said, "We'll do blueberry pancakes for her second Christmas."

We.

God, I loved that word, even though Cam surely wasn't being literal. He didn't mean anything by it.

Still, I couldn't stop smiling. "No biggie. She's not even on solid foods yet." I lifted her and asked, "Would madam like the formula or the formula?" Cora whined and blew a spit bubble. "Ah, excellent choice."

She caught sight of the Christmas tree, reaching for it and kicking as I finally got up. "Isn't that pretty?" I asked her. "It's the most perfect tree I've ever seen."

"Come on, now." Cam shook his head, but he

was clearly pleased.

Before diaper time, I had to kiss him again.

"Shh—" I broke off.

"Shucks?" Cam suggested from where he fried bacon on the hot plate. "Shhh-ugar?"

I laughed weakly, and Cam's shrewd gaze found me. All traces of teasing had vanished. "What?" he asked plainly.

"Almost out of formula. We need to get to town tomorrow."

The idea of leaving settled in my stomach like a lump of coal as I warmed Cora's bottle and monitored her tummy time on the carpet. Toby had been released outside to frolic in the early morning light.

The list of responsibilities and chores ticked through my mind. It was like we'd been inside a snow globe in Cam's cabin, but now the snow had settled and the sky was clear. The real world was crowding in.

"I need to get the car towed to town. Get settled in my—the basement apartment. Do laundry. So much laundry. Get groceries. There'll be nothing there." My heart sank with each word.

Cam was silent so long I thought he might not have heard me. Then he said flatly, "I'm going to ride out this morning to check on the herd. Give Bonnie some exercise. Tomorrow, I'll take you and Cora to the big house on Bonnie and drive you to the car. Mr. Pinter has a hitch I can borrow for the tow."

I swallowed hard. "Okay."

"Unless you want to leave today?"

"No!" I almost shouted. "I just mean…" I was about to launch into an over-explanation but stopped. "No. I don't want to leave today."

A smile tugged up Cam's lips as he flipped the sizzling bacon and Toby scratched at the door. "Good. After all, it's Christmas. They still need time to plow the roads."

Soon, with stomachs full of bacon and eggs— and the finest formula—we bundled up and headed outside with Toby, blinking in the glare. The sun was back with a vengeance.

The snow glittered like diamonds in the sun-light, the sky above the mountaintops a deep blue I hadn't seen in weeks. I inhaled the fresh air gratefully.

"Wow," I whispered, glad I'd strapped Cora into the carrier facing outward. She kicked her feet in her snowsuit.

Cam had begun trudging through the drifts to get his snow blower from the shed, but he stopped and asked, "What?"

"This." I waved my hand at the vista that

seemed to go on forever. "I took it for granted growing up."

He was silent for a moment. "Yeah. Guess I still do." He returned to stand beside me. Our breath plumed in the cold air as we gazed over the land.

We didn't move. Cora babbled against my chest, Toby running and playing, circling back to us every so often. I stared at the mountains as a swell of emotion burst up.

"It's so fucking good to be home." My eyes burned, and I couldn't blame it on the cold, dry air. "I never, ever wanted to come back after my parents were gone. I didn't realize how much I missed this."

Cam rested his big gloved hand on my shoulder and listened.

"I made the right choice, bringing Cora back. I'm so relieved we're here. Especially since we're with you."

Cam watched me. He seemed to be waiting for me to say more.

I plunged forward. "Not because you literally saved our lives—although also for that! But because we got to spend this time together. I'm grateful."

His Adam's apple bobbed. "Me too."

"I've been alone." What was I even saying? I palmed Cora's head, her hat soft under my glove.

"No, not alone. I'm with her twenty-four seven. And I love her so much."

My breath caught. "I never thought I could love anyone or anything like this. But being with you has reminded me that I want more. I *need* more. For myself. I don't know how it's only been three days, because I feel like I've known you forever. And I realize I used to know you when we were kids, but I'm so grateful to have met you again. And I'd really like to—can we still see you sometimes?"

For a second, I was afraid Cam wasn't going to reply to my word-vomit confession. I quickly added, "I know you're busy out here. No pressure."

Cam cupped my cheek, kissing me tenderly, the cold leather of his glove welcome on my hot face. His answer was a warm whisper on my lips.

"*Yes.*"

With an ominous rumble, Cora farted and pooped.

Cam and I laughed through our kiss, and he straightened, wrinkling his nose. "How can someone so tiny smell like *that*?"

"And that's coming from a rancher. Did you hear that, Cora?"

She farted again.

Tomorrow, we'd go back to the real world, and hopefully, Cam and I could see where our new connection would go. We could talk on the actual phone like it was the eighties or something.

Tomorrow, we'd leave our snow globe. But today, we had Christmas with Cam.

Chapter Eleven

JAKE

THE BASEBOARD HEATER was warm, and Cora was snug as a bug in her drawer, her beautiful face peaceful in sleep. Cam had played with her for ages, asking me questions about tummy time and getting down with her on the rug.

Watching them together made me… Well, it made me feel all sorts of things I shouldn't have. But it was Christmas, so I let myself revel in the joy and cheer and peace on Earth—and most of all, the hope.

With Cora settled for a nap on the bathroom floor—still better than a barn, right?—I flicked off the light and pulled the door halfway.

And I couldn't keep my eyes off Cam's bed. Couldn't stop thinking about what we might do in said bed. That rhymed, which made me want to giggle.

"Jake?"

I snapped my gaze to Cam, who watched me from the kitchen sink with a furrowed brow. "Yeah?" I asked too breathily.

"You look…" He shook his head. "Never mind. Are you tired?"

I nodded because I was always tired now. I had months of sleep debt accumulated.

"Okay. Get some rest."

Oh.

On one hand, I could gratefully collapse into Cam's bed and sleep. But on the other…

I peeked back through the partly open bathroom door. In a band of orange light, Cora slept soundly, her pink lips parted. Toby was out in the barn, so Cam and I were almost alone.

"Don't you want to sleep?" Cam asked, drying his hands on a tea towel.

"Yes, but no." I rubbed my face. "I'm not sure if—" I broke off. Why was this so hard? I'd been with plenty of people before. I wasn't some blushing virgin.

But what if I did or said the wrong thing? God, I really was exhausted. Outside of feeding and diapers and bath time and feeding and diapers and bath time—who even was I now?

Cam switched off the overhead light, the glow from the fire casting shadows over his bearded face. The sun was already low in the afternoon sky, the day fading through the small window.

Cam's eyes glittered, though. He crossed the distance to me slowly. Steadily. With the warmth of the fire behind me and Cam's bulk in front, I had no place to go.

And the knots of tension in my body released.

"Do you want me to tell you what to do?" Cam murmured.

Along with the sweet balm of relief, excitement sizzled through me. I nodded eagerly.

"Take off your clothes and get into bed."

With a last glance at Cora asleep, I did as I was told. The flannel sheets were soft on my bare skin as I slipped under the covers, safe and warm in Cam's bed. I watched him undress, part of me still amazed that this confident, sexy cowboy was really *Cam*.

The bed creaked as he joined me, and I was about to make a dumb joke asking if the frame was strong enough to hold both of us when he rolled on top of me.

"Oh, *fuck*," I gasped. With Cam's full weight pressing me down for the first time, my dick swelled. Instead of suffocating, it was the ultimate comfort. He was hard muscle and warm flesh, and I wanted every part of him against my skin.

"Don't you mean *fudge*?"

"Not right now, I don't."

From the bathroom, Cora grunted and made

one of her little groans. I sighed. "I should check on her."

Pressing a meaty hand on my chest, Cam straddled my hips and sat up. He craned his neck. "She's sleeping," he whispered. "You can relax."

I almost laughed. Relax? What even was relaxation? I could barely remember.

"I said *relax*." Cam circled my nipple with his thumb, still holding me down.

The guilt reared up like a horse trying to throw its rider, but I reminded myself Cam was in charge. I forced a breath and exhaled.

"That's it," he murmured, still circling with his thumb.

Cam lowered himself over me again, shifting down and replacing his thumb with his tongue. Slowly, steadily, he teased that one nipple. Sparks of pleasure danced across my skin, and I bit my lip to stop from crying out when he twisted my other nipple without warning.

My hard cock was trapped against his hairy chest. The weight and friction as he shifted made my balls tingle. I whined as he lifted to reach into the drawer under the reading lamp on the wall.

A chuckle rumbling through his chest, Cam returned, his hot, hard cock brushing my stomach. Beside me, pushing up on his left elbow, he watched me carefully.

"You still want me to tell you what to do?" he

asked in a low whisper that made me want to moan.

My mouth was dry. "Yes," I croaked.

"You can say no at any point."

I nodded.

He uncapped a bottle of lube and slicked the fingers on his right hand, watching me. Heart thudding, I nodded again. I'd do anything Cam wanted. The thought of him inside me was intimidating—but thrilling.

"I'm not going to fuck you today," Cam murmured.

Heat flushed my face. It made sense—I wasn't sure I was ready for that since I hadn't experimented much with anal. But I also wasn't sure whether or not to be disappointed.

Lips at my ear, he ordered, "Spread your legs."

Biting back a moan, I did, and he moved to kneel between them. One of his fingers circled my hole, and my thighs trembled.

In the flickering firelight, Cam watched me as he pushed a finger inside. I arched my back, squeezing my eyes shut. I flailed with hands, the pressure and stretch so sweet. My fingers dug into his shoulder, and when I opened my eyes, he was still watching me.

The intensity of his stare made my heart skip. Part of me wanted to close my eyes again and focus only on the incredible sensations of Cam finger-fucking me.

But I couldn't look away.

Under the covers in the darkening stillness of the cabin, the stove warming our skin, the intimacy as Cam pushed a second finger inside me was almost too much. Our breath gusted warm and harsh between us, the only sound aside from the crackle of wood burning.

This wasn't the distracted, perfunctory sex I'd gotten used to with Anna as the years passed, or the drunken getting off at the end of the night in university with whoever happened to be there when the party finished. It wasn't like the few hookups I'd had last year either. There was no extraneous "*oh, baby*" or other porn talk.

Not that those were bad things, but I wasn't sure I'd ever experienced sex like this. The stretch in my ass was on the knife's edge of painful, and I rocked my hips, wanting more.

Our eyes were locked together, and we were *present* in a way that made my eyes burn. My breath hitched.

Don't you dare cry again!

Nostrils flaring, Cam swooped down to kiss me, his tongue in my mouth mimicking the thrust of his fingers. I groaned into his kiss, unbearably grateful that he was in control.

When he eased back and then crooked his callused finger against just the right spot, I sucked in a breath to shout.

Cam was ready for me.

His warm, meaty hand clapped over my mouth. I groaned, trembling—then cried out against his palm as he moved back to the edge of the bed on his knees and swallowed my cock.

Sensation overwhelmed me. Cam's finger inside stroking my prostate, his wet, incredible mouth sucking my dick, his hand heavy over my mouth. I grunted and shook, pleasure building, building…

Lips glossy with spit and precum, Cam lifted his head enough to say, "I want you to come for me."

He barely had his mouth back over me when I did what he asked, moaning against the damp skin of his palm, my whole body jerking as he swallowed my load. Waves of pleasure burned through me, blood rushing in my ears.

I was absolutely wrung out, but as Cam took his leaking cock in hand and stroked, I reached for him. "Please let me," I whispered, scooting down and maneuvering us until he was on his back and I had him in my mouth.

The need to please him and make it perfect had me tensing. I sucked desperately, my lips stretching over his thick shaft, wanting to take every inch even though I choked. Cam threaded his fingers through my hair, easing me back and guiding me.

I realized I'd dug my fingers into his hips, and I relaxed my grip, reaching down for his balls. They were heavy and hairy, and I pulled off his cock to lap them. He came suddenly, splashing his belly, his fingers tightening in my hair.

Panting again, I sat up, watching Cam milk himself. I reached for his wet skin, but hesitated.

"You want to taste?" he asked gruffly.

I nodded.

"Lick it up."

With a fresh burst of desire shuddering through me, I lapped at his hairy stomach, tasting musk and rubbing my body against his legs. I moved slowly upward as Cam caressed my shoulders and head. I hadn't felt so close to another person in a very long time.

Taking my face in his rough hands, he kissed me lazily, the taste of both of us mixing on our tongues. He was warm and solid beneath me, and he urged my head down to his chest, tucking the covers around me and holding me close.

"I should check on her," I mumbled against his pecs, hair tickling my cheek.

"Go to sleep."

Guilt surged predictably, and I squirmed against him. Cam sighed and let me up. Naked, I tiptoed past the warm hearth and peeked into the bathroom. Cora slept, one arm over her head, her chest rising and falling.

"While you're up, can you let Toby in?" Cam whispered.

The floor grew cold by the door, and I hurried to tug it open. As I did, shivering in the blast of Arctic air, Cam whistled softly. Toby rocketed over from the direction of the barn, waiting obediently on the mat while I closed the door. I brushed any lingering dry snow from his fur with the towel Cam kept in the closet.

Before I could get back into bed, Toby bounded up and took my place. I stopped in my tracks, rubbing the goosebumps on my arms. I eyed the bedroll at the foot of the bed with a sigh. "No room at the inn. I can take the floor."

With a rumble of laughter, Cam gave Toby a shove and told me, "Get back here."

I snuggled back under the covers, and Cam pulled me against him, urging my head to his broad chest. Cam was like a furnace, and I pressed against him gratefully while Toby huffed and squeezed in on top of our feet. I didn't mind the crowding at all.

I wished Cora could join us. I was so afraid of rolling over on her, and with her bassinet stowed in the car, she was safer in her drawer and already fast asleep for the moment. At least she had been a minute ago. Was she still okay?

I sat up, squinting into the bathroom. With a

big hand cupping my head, Cam pulled me back to his chest. "Go. To. Sleep. She's dreaming."

The guilty tension faded away, and I let myself dream for a few minutes too…

Later, Cam made dinner while I played peeka-boo with Cora, making her laugh and kick.

I asked, "Is it cool if I put on some music?"

Stirring a chopped onion in a frying pan, Cam said, "Sure." He was making a black bean and ground beef hash, and it already smelled delicious.

I picked up my phone and hesitated. "It's not cool music or anything. I downloaded a playlist of Christmas songs for Cora."

Brow furrowed, he looked over. "Since when was I ever cool?"

I laughed. "True. Actually, do you know what a playlist is? You're living out here in the land technology forgot. Will your new house have Wi-Fi? Because I need it." The moment I spoke, I realized how presumptuous that sounded. "Not that it matters what I want! It's your house. You might not want Wi-Fi."

I turned on the playlist while Cam stirred the sizzling onions. I scrolled to "Away in a Manger," which felt right. I was struck by a memory of singing the carol in church choir as a kid with my parents watching from the pews.

I couldn't remember the words, but I hummed and joined Cam in the kitchen as the onions released a deliciously sweet scent. I pressed a kiss to his furry cheek, reminding myself not to worry about tomorrow. Tonight was Christmas, and we were safe and warm and together.

Shaking a carefully measured teaspoon of some kind of spice over the onions, Cam smiled and simply said, "I'll have Wi-Fi," and I fell in love with him even more.

Chapter Twelve

CAM

EVERY BUMP AND sway had me cringing as we made our way to the big house. I'd done the journey on Bonnie a thousand times—but never with a baby strapped to my chest.

Not just any baby, but the best, most special little girl in the world. Not that I'd known any other babies, but... Yes, she was clearly the *best* baby. Was it possible to fall in love in three days? Because the tenderness I felt for Cora was unlike anything I'd ever known.

Not to mention what I felt for her daddy.

The teenage crush I'd had on Jake felt feather-light and insignificant. As powerful as it had been back then, compared to now? Now, when Jake pressed against me, his hands hooked around my hips, head nudging my Stetson. Trusting me to carry his baby.

Now, when I wanted to keep riding to the horizon with Jake and Cora and not let them go.

As we climbed over a rise and the big house appeared in the distance, I reminded myself that it had been *three damn days*. Sure, this was day four, but that didn't exactly help my case. I needed to screw my head on straight. I had a ton of work to do, and Jake and Cora couldn't just stay with me forever.

I'd never even really had a boyfriend, and now I was chewing over the idea of forever?

Fool.

"Where's your new house?" Jake asked.

"To the east. Built a new road on the property." I'd spotted the roof earlier but hadn't said anything. It was best to get Jake and Cora to Lonely Creek. I didn't want her to be outside for too long.

My truck was parked in a secondary freestanding garage near the stable at the big house, and I hoped we could drop off Bonnie and scoot away unnoticed. 'Course we weren't even to the stable yet when the familiar shape of Hal Jr. appeared on the porch.

The big house was a sprawling wood, stone, and glass mansion. Not a fancy design, but huge with seven bedrooms and even more bathrooms. The porch was covered and wide with a line of rocking chairs.

A few years older than me, Hal was on the short side like his dad, wearing his cowboy hat and boots like he had something to prove. A face only a mother could love, though I supposed I was being unfair. It was his personality that ruined his average looks.

I had no clue how he'd landed his wife Shelby—blond, bubbly, and deserved far better. She joined him outside, zipping her puffy, goose down coat as they approached.

"Merry Christmas!" Shelby called. "And happy Boxing Day. I just spent way too much saving twenty-five percent on a European blender." Her eyes lit up. "That *is* a baby! Who's this?"

"Since when do you have a baby?" Hal asked—demanded.

Jake dismounted before I carefully hopped down from Bonnie, keeping a hand on Cora. He said, "This is my daughter, Cora. Cam rescued us from Coyote Trail just before the storm arrived. Saved our lives."

Shelby gasped. "Oh, my goodness. How did you even know that old road was there?"

"I grew up in Lonely Creek."

Hal's eyes narrowed. "You were that baseball player. I didn't know you two were…friends."

He watched us, hands shoved in his pockets, Stetson pulled low. All he needed was chewing tobacco. He'd grown up on the ranch fair and square, but after years away, he had the air of a city slicker playing dress-up.

Shelby's smile turned brittle as she glared at her husband. "Why shouldn't they be?" She stuck out her gloved hand to Jake. "Shelby Pinter. Lovely to meet you. And this is Cora, you said? Oh, I miss having a baby around. Our youngest is five now."

Standing close, Jake took her out of the carrier, raising his eyebrows at me in silent question, undoubtedly sensing the tension between me and Hal.

As Shelby cooed over Cora in Jake's arms, I told Hal, "I'm going to borrow the hitch to tow Jake's car into town."

"Does my father know about this?"

I kept my tone steady and tried not to clench my jaw. "He's still out of the country as far as I know."

Before Hal could go into full jackass mode, Shelby said, "Of course your dad wouldn't mind lending the hitch. Cam, you know where it is?"

"Yes, ma'am," I drawled, tipping my hat to her. "I'll grab it and we'll be out of your hair."

It was easy for me to get under Hal's skin just by talking to Shelby, which made no sense since he knew I was gay. I looped Bonnie's reins over my wrist and turned to the stable.

Shelby asked, "Have you been to your house?

The foreman couldn't get a hold of you. He said to tell you they only need a couple more days. You'll have the keys by New Year's Eve for sure."

"Dunno why you built it so small," Hal said. "But I guess that's how you grew up. Not to mention the shack you've been living in out there." He laughed heartily, like we were all in on the joke.

I said, "Thanks, Shel," and turned on my heel, gravel crunching under my boots beneath the thin layer of snow left by the plow. Jake followed, carrying Cora, who babbled happily in his arms.

It was really happening. The house had taken so long to build that there'd been times I hadn't believed it actually would be. Always one delay after another, but now it was almost mine.

I should have been thrilled, but the task of dropping off Jake and Cora in town felt like a storm cloud hanging heavy and low.

In the barn, I got Bonnie settled while Cora cooed at all the new sights and smells.

Jake's voice rose and took on that sweet, sing-song quality as he pointed. "There's another horsey like Bonnie. That's a horseshoe. Over there is hay and a rake. Oh, and a big pile of poop." He snorted, his octave returning to normal. "You'll be quite familiar with that."

I chuckled as I fed Bonnie an apple, my shoulders relaxing. When she was finished chomping, I couldn't resist going over to Jake and giving Cora a smile and making a funny face, which had her kicking and squealing. I could have spent hours sticking out my tongue and watching her reactions. Were babies always this…addictive?

"What's the deal with that dude?" Jake asked. "I don't remember him."

"Doesn't like me much." I gasped and made wide eyes at Cora, wiggling my fingers. My chest tightened. It was so easy to make her happy.

Jake laughed. "Yeah, I picked up on that."

"He spent his childhood wishing he was somewhere else. But when his father took me on and took a liking to me, Hal Jr. got jealous, I guess." I tore myself away from Cora and petted Bonnie's muzzle, making sure she got her fair share of attention. "Dunno how the Pinters raised such a turd of a man."

"At least his wife is nice." Jake bounced Cora, making her giggle so sweetly. "Hey, can we see the new house? You said they built a road?"

Why did it make me nervous? That didn't make a lick of sense. But it would delay taking them back to Lonely Creek, so I said, "Sure."

Shelby appeared in the doorway. "Do you need a car seat? Lori and Hal Sr. had one for when they babysat the kids." She held it up. "Should go on the passenger side just fine, Cam. Be sure to deactivate the air bag, and Jake'll have to squish into the middle."

It hadn't occurred to me, and Jake exhaled in a rush and said, "Shh—*oot*, I didn't even think about it! Thank you so much. Wow. I need to engage my brain."

Shelby gave him a kind smile. "It's okay. That's what mommas are for."

Jake's smile stretched too thin, but he took the car seat with more thanks. "I'm still new to this. I guess I was focusing on getting into town, not the logistics."

Is he eager to get into town?

With a mental headshake, I told myself I was being even more of a fool reading too much into every word out of Jake's mouth.

To her credit, Shelby didn't ask any nosy questions about where Cora's mother might be. In the garage, Jake installed the seat on the passenger side of my truck while I held Cora against my chest, swaying slightly. She was so very *small*, and I tried not to think about how many ways the world could hurt her.

As Jake struggled with a twisted seat belt, tension creasing his face and lifting his shoulders, I said, "It's okay."

He sighed, sagging against the door. "It's hard not to feel guilty that it didn't even cross my mind. Of *course* we need a car seat to take her in the truck!"

"This isn't a normal situation. You did your best. You're doing your best. You're a great dad. A great parent."

Jake sighed again, this time with a soft smile. "Thank you." He watched me, and seemed about to say something else. Finally, he said, "Let's see this house of yours."

It wasn't sprawling like the big house, but my two-story home was built of the same timber, stone, and glass. There was a separate garage and a stable and paddock behind. The house faced the snow-capped Rockies, with a soaring great room window that took up most of the wall.

There were four bedrooms, which seemed like three too many, but the Pinters had convinced me it was a good idea to have guest rooms for my mom and... Well, that was about it. Wasn't like the yaks were going to bunk in.

"Oh, wow!" Jake exclaimed as we neared, pressed against my side in the middle seat. "*Wow.* Cam, this is incredible!"

My chest was tight with pride, which was foolish since it wasn't like I built the place myself. There were several pickups parked outside, and drilling and hammering echoed from inside.

"I guess it's really happening," I said. "I'm going to live here."

"*Yeah*, you are. I mean, the cabin has its charms, but this is gorgeous." Jake craned his head around. "That view!"

I shrugged and stopped the truck, feeling strangely bashful.

"I'm so happy for you." Jake took my bare hand and squeezed it. "You deserve it." Beside us, Cora grunted and gurgled, and Jake said, "Cora agrees, obviously."

I gripped his fingers, not wanting to let go.

"So, we can come over when you're all moved in?"

All I said was, "Yeah," when I wanted to beg them to stay. I put the truck in park and hurried in to talk to the foreman, who gave me the keys and told me it would be all mine December thirty-first.

By the time we made it into Lonely Creek hauling Jake's broken Ford behind us, the afternoon was getting long in the tooth. I'd have to ride Bonnie to the cabin in the dark, but that was nothing new.

"Left here," Jake said, directing me to the house he'd grown up in.

Cora was asleep, and he'd gone quiet beside me, looking around as we passed through town, surely cataloging all the differences. There weren't many to my eye, but I probably hadn't noticed the slow changes over the years.

"Stackers is still here," he murmured. "Pancakes still good?"

"Dunno. Haven't been there in years."

"Bet they have blueberry. We should go." He quickly added, "I mean, if you want."

"That'd be good."

"Cool."

A strange tension filled the cab, my mouth dry as I pulled up to the curb where Jake pointed. He gazed at the house, which was a one-story ranch style. Made of brown brick, its roof was snow-covered and lights blazed from the windows in the fading afternoon.

Adam's apple bobbing, Jake stared at the house he'd known so many years ago. I could imagine his memories of his parents and the life he'd had as a kid. I snaked my arm behind and squeezed his shoulders.

"The door used to be just brown," he said roughly. "Red is good. Looks good. I'm sure the basement reno will be great."

I could hear thumping, and as a young man exited from the side door, music spilled out. The guy grabbed a case of beer from the snow and returned inside.

Jake smiled thinly. "Guess we should expect noise with a vacation rental. People come to ski and party. It's fine."

My gut twisted. Words tangled in my head.

He said, "Anyway, we should get inside. Unpack." He turned to me, still trying to smile. "Thank you. You really made our Christmas incredible. It wasn't my first like Cora's, but I'll never forget it."

"I miss you already," I blurted.

Jake blinked at me, then licked his lips. "Okay," he said tentatively.

"I don't want you to leave. Don't want to see you once in a while, and maybe more will come of it and maybe not. I want more *now*. I want you."

Jake's breath was shallow. "And Cora?" He glanced at her.

She was still sleeping, the sweep of her thick eyelashes fanned over her pink cheeks.

I didn't have to think about it. "Yes."

"Are you sure?" He smiled tentatively.

"I've never been more sure of anything."

"After only a few days?"

"Don't know how to explain it, but yes."

Jake gripped my thigh. "We'll be fine here. I don't want you to feel guilty or something."

"I don't. But I also don't want either of you staying here." As punctuation, the thudding bass of a new song practically shook the truck. "Even if this was a perfect mansion, I'd still want you to come back to the cabin with me."

Jake opened and closed his mouth. I could see the hope shining in his beautiful brown eyes. "But... You'll change your mind. You can't really want us to *move in*. You'll get home tonight and be glad for the peace and quiet."

"I'll get home tonight and miss you both."

Jake's exhale gusted out. He bit his lip, and I wanted to kiss him senseless more than anything in the whole world.

He said, "There's not enough room. You'll— "

"My house will be ready this week. There'll be more room than I know what to do with. Move in with me."

"We just re-met! It's been less than a week. We can't."

"Says who?" The godawful music hammered my skull.

"Uh, everyone? What if it doesn't work out? If...*we* don't?"

I shrugged. "Then move out."

Jake laughed. "I mean, it sounds logical when you put it like that, but—holy shit, how is that music this *loud*?" He looked at Cora, who was somehow still asleep. "I... I don't want to do the wrong thing."

"You don't have to stay with me. You can leave whenever you want."

"Right." I could practically see the gears turning in his head. "And if you decide it's not working, just tell me, and we'll leave. We have to promise to be honest with each other."

I nodded.

Jake exhaled a shaky breath, looking between me and Cora before gazing at me seriously. "You really want to be with me? With us? Your peaceful life won't be the same."

I imagined returning to the cabin alone. Seeing the Christmas tree by the hearth and the duct-taped lights around the ceiling. My chair waiting for me. I could stoke the fire and read my book with Toby at my feet. Have an early night before I returned to long days on the land with my yaks and Mr. Pinter's cattle.

Go back to my "peaceful life."

"It'll be so damn lonely without you and Cora."

Jake exhaled a sort of whimper and kissed me, holding my face. "Oh, Cam. Maybe we're kidding ourselves."

I nuzzled his cheek. "Peaceful doesn't have to mean quiet. It would be a new kind of peace." Lungs tight, I asked, "What do you think?"

Jake's lips tugged up into a small, perfect smile. "Tell me what to do."

Chapter Thirteen

CAM

STEPPING BACK, JAKE and I eyed the crib critically. He grasped the railing and shook it violently, but the crib didn't move an inch.

"I think it's good," I said.

"What do *you* think?" Jake asked a sleepy Cora in that singsong voice he reserved strictly for her.

It always made me smile. Granted, it had only been just over a week, so maybe I'd get tired of it.

I didn't think so.

Picking Cora up from her car seat on the floor, Jake lowered her into the crib as I adjusted the video monitor. Receiver in hand, I crossed the hall to the principal bedroom.

There was no furniture yet, and since it was New Year's Eve, there wouldn't be any for days. The overhead light fixture was black iron in a swirling pattern made by a local craftsman. It cast shadows on the warm, white walls. Everything felt too clean and big and echoey, but I knew we'd fill the space soon and scuff it up.

I set the receiver on a cardboard box by the big, dark window, and the crib filled the screen.

"It works!" I called.

On the screen, Jake straightened from where he'd leaned over Cora, tucking her into new sheets and a blanket. "Yeah?"

He disappeared on the monitor and reappeared in the doorway a few moments later. Crouching beside me, he peered at the screen. "The Wi-Fi signal's great."

It hadn't been easy, but I'd made sure the phone line and internet were installed on time. It didn't matter to me, but it mattered to Jake.

He smiled at the screen. "She seems out for the count. Going to miss midnight."

"Join the club." I checked my watch to find it was just after nine. "I haven't stayed up for New Year's Eve since I was a kid."

Jake yawned. "Last year, I was at a club in downtown Toronto getting drunk. Feels like someone else's life."

I'd only seen nightclubs in movies. "Miss it?" Why was I holding my breath? He'd lived in the city for years. This was a hell of a change.

He smiled at Cora on the monitor, then leaned in and kissed me. "Nope," he murmured against my lips.

Exhaling, I slid my tongue into his welcoming mouth, reaching up to cup his head. Every kiss brought a rush of blood, the excitement more than physical. I still couldn't believe I was kissing anyone, let alone *Jake*. I reckoned the thrill would wear off eventually, but I hoped not.

Pulling back, Jake said, "Although I wouldn't mind a drink. Guess we don't have any bubbly on hand."

"Sorry. I have the odd beer in summer, but that's about it. I can call over to the big house. I'm sure Shelby has something she wouldn't mind parting with."

"Nah. Not worth having to deal with Hal Jr. Besides, I haven't had anything in months. If I start drinking now, it'll go straight to my head and we'll never get that mattress upstairs."

I'd rile Hal Jr. all day if it meant making Jake happy. "I can handle the mattress on my own."

"Oh, can you?" A teasing smile lit up Jake's face. "Okay, let's see you try."

Fine, wrestling the king-sized mattress around the bend in the stairs was easier said than done.

"Pivot!" Jake yelled from a few stairs below. "Pivot!"

He whistled and clapped, and I strained to bend the firm mattress just enough to squeeze it around the bend.

"Want a hand yet, big man?" Jake asked.

With a laugh, I surrendered.

My socks slipped a bit on the shiny new hardwood as I tugged and Jake pushed, and I made a mental note to buy one of those carpets that went down the middle of a staircase. Before we knew it, Cora would be walking, and I had to make sure she didn't fall.

A voice in my head piped up and said that I was getting ahead of myself, but I shushed it.

Sure, maybe it wouldn't work out with me and Jake. But as we dropped the mattress onto the floor in the bedroom and Jake toppled me onto it, being with him felt *right*. A truth in my bones I couldn't deny.

The plastic wrap on the mattress crinkled under us as we flopped out. "Good thing the box spring's not here yet," I said. "That's enough of going up and down those stairs." It had been a long day of tending my herd and moving bits and pieces from the cabin on the ATV.

"I hate to break it to you that the truck's not empty yet."

"It can wait 'til next year."

With the plastic rustling, Jake rolled into me, one leg over mine. "Guess we can have an early night." He spread his hand over my plaid shirt, his fingers sneaking in between buttons to tease my skin. "*Although*... We could christen your new mattress first."

"Our mattress."

Jake's face flushed as he grinned, and I pulled him down for a long, slow kiss. As it deepened, I rolled him under me, the squeaking plastic loud in the empty room.

We laughed, and Jake said, "Guess we should get the sheets out of the dryer. Who knows where this plastic's been."

Groaning, I nodded, and we hurried downstairs for the necessities. Toby was still outside, and I made sure his dog door was clear of snow. I grabbed my toiletries and rooted around for the lube while Jake wrestled the new fitted sheet onto the mattress.

I'd gone with a simple navy sheet set and duvet cover in the highest thread count since Shelby had told me the higher the better. I'd picked out sheets and blankets for the crib as well after Jake had stood in the linen aisle at the home store in Lethbridge reading packages for almost half an hour, getting more and more tense.

We stripped off, and then Jake examined the monitor, bending over and giving me a great view of his ass. I knew he was anxious about sleeping in a different room and transitioning Cora to a crib, but he'd talked about healthy boundaries and parenting studies and statistics.

I pushed the mattress against the wall and

spread out on it. We'd grabbed the pillows downstairs, and I propped my head up, watching him. "She okay?" I asked quietly.

Jake straightened and stepped back. "Yep. Fast asleep." He bent again and turned the box so the screen angled away. "Just gonna…" He stepped back. "I'll still hear her if she cries."

"Yep."

"The volume's up, right?" He bent and pressed buttons and waited. "I don't hear anything."

With a grunt, I rolled to my feet and padded naked down the hall to the half-dark nursery. A mushroom nightlight glowed near the crib. "Hear me?" I whispered before going back to our room.

Jake nodded and slipped his arms around my waist. "Thank you. Sorry."

"Don't be." I leaned our foreheads together.

"Now, where were we?" Jake nudged me toward the mattress, and I walked backward.

Stretched out on my back, I inhaled sharply with a bolt of desire as Jake straddled my hips. Then he glanced to the huge window, his eyes widening.

"Wait, we need curtains!"

"No one around for miles, city slicker."

"Oh, right. Duh." He grinned down at me. "Well?"

"Well, what?"

The corners of Jake's eyes crinkled as he spoke

slowly and surely. "Tell me what to do."

"Hmm." I rubbed my hands over his strong, hairy thighs. "Dunno where to start." Tugging him closer, I reached around to caress the crack of his ass. "Did you like it when I put my fingers inside you?"

Jake nodded eagerly.

"Think you can take my cock?"

Eyes widening, his breath caught. He nodded again.

I traced my fingertips up and down his crack, skimming his hole. On one hand, I wanted to watch him ride me. See him flex and work to take me inch by inch while his prick hardened…

But as the seconds passed, his expression flickered, some of the excited confidence evaporating. I could practically see him start to overthink, his gaze flicking to the monitor, his hands fidgeting on my waist.

In one powerful movement, I rolled Jake under me. "Spread your legs."

Moaning, his eyes closing, Jake did.

I took my time lubing his ass, finger-fucking him in long, steady strokes until he was quivering.

"Please, Cam. Fuck me."

Some kind of animal instinct swelled in me. "Say it again."

"Fuck me," he moaned, sweat beading on his forehead and dampening his wavy hair.

"My name."

"Oh!" Jake smiled. "Cam. *Cam.*"

As I pushed my cock inside, I could tell he was holding his breath—along with squeezing his eyes shut so tightly I worried for his eyeballs. I stilled and nuzzled his cheek.

"It's okay. I'm here with you."

"Kind of hard to forget," Jake gritted out. He opened his eyes, and we laughed. "Dude, that really was a hell of a growth spurt you had after high school."

I could feel him relaxing, and I pushed in another inch with a smile. "Haven't had any complaints 'til now."

"Not complaining, just—" Jake gasped, his back arching. "Oh, f—"

"Fiddlesticks? Fudge? Fooey?" I retreated a few inches back and then in farther.

"*Fuck*," Jake breathed, his Adam's apple bobbing and head tipped back.

"Mmm." I leaned down to kiss his stubbly throat, licking at the fresh, salty drops of sweat gathered in the hollow.

"Haven't done this in a long time," Jake rasped. Our eyes met, and he sucked in a breath, hands clutching my back around my ribs. "Feels like the first time."

As I pushed another inch inside, I captured his mouth in a wet, messy kiss. "You're mine," I practically growled.

Jake made soft, desperate little noises in the back of his throat. Even though he wasn't that much smaller, a flood of protectiveness filled me, rushing through my veins like blood.

I'd fucked men over the years, but not like this. This was…*more*, and suddenly it was me tensing and short of breath. I'd definitely never fucked raw before, and Christ, the incredible heat of being inside him with nothing between us had my balls tightening.

I didn't give a shit if it was too fast. We trusted each other. And that it was Jake Gregson of all people that my heart and soul and bones had decided to trust didn't feel surprising anymore.

Right was right, and I wasn't going to waste my breath arguing with it.

When I was all the way inside, I reached down and touched Jake's stretched hole. "You're taking all of me."

"I love it."

With a teasing smile, I rocked gently. "You sure?"

"Uh-huh."

Jake's teeth flashed white, his laugh a little strained.

"Too much?" He was tight as hell around me, and I had to be heavy on top of him.

"No!" He grabbed at my hip and shoulder.

"Stay. I love how big you are. It feels so good, like, like the rest of the world's gone. It's just you and me." His expression creased, and he turned his head toward the monitor. "I don't mean—I—"

"It's okay." I turned his face back to me, gazing into his eyes. "Right now, it's only you and me, and that's okay. You're allowed. You're safe. We're all safe."

Eyes filling with tears, Jake nodded and pulled me down for a long, desperate kiss.

"Now take my cock the way you're meant to."

Groaning, Jake nodded and raked his blunt nails over my arms, his legs wide as I fucked him. The slapping of our flesh echoed in the empty room, and my muscles strained.

Jake was hard between us, his back arching and cock red and glistening. He gasped as I wrapped a slick hand around him.

I didn't have to tell him to come for me.

As Jake shook and squeezed around me, I thrust harder. Panting, he watched me fuck him, lips parted, nodding. When he reached up and circled my nipples, I came inside him, my whole body on fire.

We stayed wet and tangled together until our breathing returned to normal. I tugged the new duvet over us, my eyes heavy…

When I woke after a doze, the room was dark aside from the low light of the baby monitor. I sat up and rubbed my face. "Jake?"

Still naked, he kneeled in front of the monitor with a sheet around him. "Sorry. I can't sleep with her in another room. I know I have to get used to it. She does too. But…" His gaze returned to the screen.

"S'okay. Next year."

Still naked, we hauled the mattress into Cora's room, shushing each other and trying not to laugh too loudly before we settled under the duvet. Cora didn't stir even as Toby bounded in, and we were all fast asleep before twelve.

At least until Cora woke us.

As she fussed in Jake's arms, midnight came and went, and our future began.

Epilogue

JAKE

One Year Later

WITH ONE EYE on the clock, I made listening noises as my client complained. Most of the time, they just wanted to be heard. We were on the phone and not a video call, so at least I didn't have to put on a shirt and tie for this meeting.

I knew exactly how to fix the issue, but I waited and let him vent. My second-floor office window overlooked the front...well, it wasn't really a *yard* when it stretched for miles.

I could see the snowy peaks of the Rockies over my monitor, and outside, I could hear Cora shrieking with delight as she played with Mrs. Pinter—Lori.

It was so tempting to stand and peek out the

window to see what was making her so happy, but I focused on my client. It was my last call of the day, and considering my boss had let me transition to part time indefinitely, I had to put in my best work.

It was the beginning of December, and the days were getting shorter and shorter. By the time I tugged on my boots and outdoor gear, the golden sunset spilled over the snow-covered land.

Lori waved, and Cora's beautiful, perfect face lit up. It wasn't windy, but the air was crisp, and her cheeks were pink.

"Dada!" Holding a red plastic spade, she ran over on her tiny legs, her bulky purple snowsuit giving her an awkward gait. She was still small for almost eighteen months, but she was hitting her milestones.

I scooped her up and pressed kisses to her cold cheeks. "Hi, sweetie." A green crocodile hat knit by Lori protected her head and covered her dark curls. They were just like mine had been in the baby album I'd found in the boxes in Uncle Steve's garage. We didn't see him or his family much, but that was fine.

I'd found my own family.

"Look!" Cora pointed her mitten-clad hand toward a pile of snow. She grinned, her cheek dimpling the way Anna's did, which I thought was a nice gift from her mother. I hadn't heard from

Anna, and I didn't expect to.

Groaning softly, Lori pushed to her feet. "Snow's not good for packing, so our castle looks more like a hill. But she's having fun."

I *oohed* and *ahhed* over the small snow mound and encouraged Cora as she filled her small plastic beach bucket again.

To Lori, I said, "Thank you. Are you sure—"

She cut me off with a firm shake of her head, her silver ponytail swaying. "I've told you and Cam a hundred times that it's my pleasure to come by whenever you need me. My grandbabies are all the way in Calgary and Edmonton. I need my fix. There's no sense in you driving her all the way into Lonely Creek for daycare when I'm right up at the big house with not enough to do. Though I'd better head back now and get dinner out of the crockpot."

We hugged, and Cora waved bye-bye to Aunt Lori. Cam and I managed our schedules weekly to split caring for Cora, and we'd arranged it so he could bring her to work sometimes, performing tasks like cleaning out the stable with her strapped to his back. But there were days when Cam had to be off on a distant part of the ranch all day.

Lori's taillights had only disappeared where the road dipped before Cam's headlights appeared. The sun was below the mountaintops, the lingering golden light bathing us.

"Bam-bam!" Cora shouted.

Cam tooted the horn as he pulled in, which made her flail with joy every single time. He parked his truck in the garage beside my SUV—a used Subaru that so far was performing far better than the Ford I'd bought in Toronto. Granted, that was a low bar.

With Cora in my arms, we met him in front of the garage. "Bam-bam!" she cried.

"Hi, sugar pie." Cam took her from me, kissing her nose and making her giggle.

For whatever reason, "Cam" had translated to "bam" in Cora's mind before evolving into "Bam-bam." We put on old *Flintstones* episodes sometimes, and she pointed to Cam every time the character of Bam-bam was mentioned.

Honestly, it suited him.

"Hey, babe." I kissed him, loving that his lips tasted of his favorite mint Chapstick. "How'd it go?" He'd been helping Hal Sr. with the cattle, so he'd taken the truck over to the big house, and Bonnie had had the day off in her paddock.

"Good. I stopped into town too." He nodded to the truck. "Give me a hand?"

I gasped as he pulled back the tarp. "I thought we were waiting a week so the tree doesn't dry out too much?"

He shrugged. "Wanted to surprise you."

The pine tree was beautiful. It was also definitely a two-person job to maneuver it inside, even with Cam's muscles. The pine smelled like heaven, even if the needles scratched.

With the tree in front of the soaring picture window in the living room, we strung the lights and hung the new decorations I'd bought along with the ones Lori had gifted Cam for the cabin.

While Toby raced around, getting under foot, Cora tried to eat the tinsel, then started knocking the ornaments off like a cat.

It was perfect.

ON CHRISTMAS MORNING, Cam woke me in the predawn darkness, spooned behind me with his erection hard against my ass. He whispered, "Roll over and let me fuck you."

"*Tell me what to do*" was often unsaid now. I wasn't overwhelmed and exhausted the way I had been a year ago, but his taking control was our secret handshake, one of the tender threads binding us. He always knew how to take care of me. How to love me.

And I loved him right back.

Suddenly awake, I got my knees under me, thighs spread. "Fuck, yes."

Cam's slick cock nudged at my hole. "That's a loonie for the swear jar," he teased.

"Make it a twoonie. So fucking—" I gasped as he slowly pushed inside me, hot and raw, "—worth it."

From the first time Cam had fucked me on the new mattress on the floor, I'd loved having him inside me. It wasn't only the delicious stretch of his cock, but the caress of his lips on my neck or cheek. The whispers of encouragement. The power and tenderness of his big hands.

"That's it," he murmured now, lips warm on my ear as he rocked inside me. "I've got you. I'm gonna make you come."

And boy, did he ever.

Downstairs, we'd left the Christmas tree lit overnight, and the rainbow glow welcomed me as I tiptoed down in the too-big reindeer onesie that I still loved wearing.

I knew Cora was still too young to really understand Santa, but I'd kept most of the presents wrapped and waiting in a garbage bag at the back of the guest room closet.

Tail wagging, Toby bounded in from the kitchen, where I had all the fixings for blueberry pancakes waiting. I bent and scratched his head, letting him lick my chin.

I'd just finished arranging the boxes and bags under the tree when Cam came down with Cora in his arms, his steps padded by the thick carpet runner on the stairs. He wore his usual sweats, T-shirt, and woolly socks, and I hoped he'd agree to wear the matching Christmas pajamas I'd gotten the three of us.

"Merry Christmas!" I cried, and Cora clapped, her eyes lighting up. "Santa was here. Look at all the presents under our tree! And he filled our—"

I blinked past the rocking chair at the three red stockings hanging from the mantel with care under the flatscreen TV. In neat white script, our names had been sewn into each:

Cora

Dada

Bam-bam

Joy flowed through me. "How? When?"

Cam lowered Cora to the rug so she could run to the tree, Toby darting around her. He shrugged, but he couldn't stop smiling, which was *adorable*.

"I had it done in town. Switched the stockings out with decoys. So now we have six, FYI."

Grinning, I traced the letters with my finger. "This is why you insisted on stuffing the stockings last night."

"Yep. Thanks for the Chapstick."

I slapped his chest lightly. "You weren't supposed to open anything!"

"I didn't! Don't tell me that tiny tube is anything else. I'm impressed that you were able to wrap it."

"I'm very skilled, and—"

We both turned at the sound of ripping paper and joined Cora and Toby before they could do too much damage.

Later, I posted a selfie in our matching PJs that Cam took with his long arm. We were laughing in front of the tree with a mess of wrapping paper and bows scattered around us, Cora in my arms and Toby licking Cam's ear. The pic was blurry and too close.

Cam offered to take another, but I didn't want to change a thing.

THE END

About the Author

Keira aims for the perfect mix of character, plot, and heat in her M/M romances. She writes everything from swashbuckling pirates to heart-warming holiday escapism. Her fave tropes are enemies to lovers, age gaps, forced proximity, and passionate virgins. Although she loves delicious angst along the way, Keira guarantees happy endings!

Discover more at:

KeiraAndrews.com

Printed in Great Britain
by Amazon

51195254R00118